SADIE THATCHER'S BIMBO HALLOWEEN ANTHOLOGY
2021

SADIE THATCHER

Copyright © 2021 by Sadie Thatcher

All rights reserved.

No part of this book may be reproduced in any form or by any electronic or mechanical means, including information storage and retrieval systems, without written permission from the author, except for the use of brief quotations in a book review.

❦ Created with Vellum

CONTENTS

BIGFOOT AND THE BIMBO

Bigfoot and the Bimbo	3

BIMBO ZERO

Bimbo Zero	25

THE LEGEND OF THE WEREBIMBO

Chapter 1	53
Chapter 2	57
Chapter 3	61
Chapter 4	65
Chapter 5	69
Chapter 6	73
Chapter 7	77
Chapter 8	81
Chapter 9	85
Chapter 10	90
Chapter 11	94
Chapter 12	98
Chapter 13	102
Chapter 14	106
About the Author	109
Also by Sadie Thatcher	111

BIGFOOT AND THE BIMBO

Taryn hiked deeper into the woods. She cut across country, having left the trail half an hour earlier. The trail did not take her where she needed to go. And with her map and compass, along with a GPS unit to back her up, Taryn was confident she would find her way.

There had been some strange reports lately from this section of the forest. Taryn was there to investigate. She spent about half of each year working as a National Park ranger, but her purpose here was very different. She was not out in the woods in any official capacity. This was purely for her own interest. Taryn was hunting for the elusive Bigfoot.

How Taryn had fallen into the world of Bigfoot research even surprised her when she looked back on it. She had always been in the right spot at the right time to get the needed information to further fuel her interest. However, it all started while she was in college, out for a run at dusk around a nearby reservoir, she thought she saw something she could not explain. The possibilities seemed to either be a tree blowing in the wind or Bigfoot. Rationally, she knew it was a tree, but that moment excited her enough to dig deeper.

What Taryn expected to find as she hiked deeper into the woods, she had no idea. The truth was she just wanted to find something that would make her trip worth it. After coming across the series of reports from the area that involved strange noises and smells, a dog that went a bit mad, and the random movement of objects at a nearby logging operation, there was enough there to warrant a search. But after a five-hour drive, Taryn wanted to make the time and effort she had already put in worth it.

The uphill climb was difficult, especially through the dense foliage. If Taryn was honest with herself, she would have questioned how a large ape-like creature could live in such a dense forest without giving off clear signs of its presence. However, she was past the point of questioning Bigfoot's existence. She just wanted to find something, anything that would give her a reward for her dedication.

"Almost to the top," Taryn told herself, urging herself upward. She could sense that she was near the top of the hill. From there, she would check her map and decide where she needed to go next.

However, the top of the hill turned out to be more like a knife-edge ridge. Either Taryn's map was wrong or she was not where she thought she was. The GPS unit was just for backup. She had been confident enough in her map and compass skills to make it a backup. Besides, she needed line of sight with satellites for her GPS unit to work and the heavy tree cover made that difficult.

Taryn took her eyes off where she was stepping for the briefest of moments, but that was all it took. Suddenly her feet were slipping out from underneath her and she was slipping down the other side of the hill. The soft earth gave way beneath her and she fell flat on her butt, but all the while sliding down the hill. She tried to grab onto something to stop her, but she could not find anything that could stop her from sliding.

"Ouch," Taryn called out when she finally stopped. Her foot got caught on a tree stump and caught. There was a crunching sound. Without the shock of pain, Taryn knew it would be bad. There was no way she would be able to hike out again. As far as she knew, she was going to be stuck for a while.

Getting hurt out in the middle of nowhere was bad enough. Taryn knew she had supplies to sustain her. She had come prepared to make camp. She had a week's worth of food in her pack. However, that knowledge did not stop the panic from rising in her throat and the tears from forming at the corners of her eyes. The only thing that could have made her injury worse was if there had been blood.

"Keep it together, Taryn," she told herself, trying to fight back against the negative thoughts that were spinning around in her head. It only helped a little bit.

Taryn looked up to see her trail she had left behind with her fall. The hill was steep back up to the ridge. Even if she had not hurt her foot and ankle, she would have struggled to climb back up that hill. And that either meant she was lost or her map was wrong.

However, before Taryn could even begin to assess her situation, the bushes around her started to rustle. There was someone or something out there.

"Hello," Taryn called out, hopeful that she had not just stumbled upon a bear or a cougar. She was not up for dealing with a predator at the moment.

The rustling stopped as soon as Taryn called out. Whoever or whatever it was, and she was leaning toward whatever, had heard her and stopped moving. Not that Taryn could make herself be completely silent. The panic and adrenaline flooding her body made her breathe heavily. Her heart pounded in her chest. Even she could hear it over the sound of her breathing. Whatever was out there could surely hear her too.

Then Taryn looked up, trying to get her bearings in case she needed to make a run for it.

"Holy fuck," Taryn called out as she came face to face with a hairy face looking down at her. She could not believe it, even after all she had hoped for. It was real. Bigfoot was real, because she was looking right up at him.

There was silence. Neither of them moved. They just looked at each other. Taryn was staring, because she could not help it, but the Bigfoot creature looking down at her blinked normally, more curious than anything. It was the strangest of encounters. It was as if two cultures of people who had never seen each other finally came face to face and neither of them knew what to do or what to say to the other.

"Language," spoke the creature in a chastising manner. The voice was deep, but the words were formed perfectly.

Taryn sat there on the ground, dumbfounded. This was real. She had to tell herself that. She was not hallucinating. Bigfoot was real. And it just talked to her, in perfect English. It did not make sense, but Taryn was past the point where anything made sense. It just was.

"You're Bigfoot?" Taryn said, her voice weak and timid. Any anger at her situation was now gone.

"That's what humans like to call me," the creature said.

His mouth moved as Taryn would have expected a human's to move, even though the creature looked far more ape-like than human. This was not someone playing a trick on her. It wasn't a man in a mask. Taryn had already been the victim of a hoax before, when a fellow National Park ranger dressed up in a gorilla costume to scare her. All it had done was make her angry and two other fellow rangers were needed to hold her back to prevent her from kicking the shit out of the gorilla costumed man.

"What do you like to call you?" Taryn asked, quickly realizing the grammar was less than stellar.

"I'm Miles," the creature said. "And I take it you're Taryn?"

For the briefest of moments, Taryn questioned how this creature knew her name, but then she remembered she had been talking to herself earlier, calling herself by her name.

"Yes, that's right," Taryn finally said. "I fell and hurt my foot or ankle. I can't tell which at the moment."

The creature calling himself Miles looked down at Taryn's foot. It was hard to see anything with all the mud and debris around her. The recent rains had made some areas of the forest quite dangerous. He then looked up the hill to see the trail Taryn had left behind from her fall. It was impressive and almost left him to wonder how Taryn had avoided further injury than a hurt foot or ankle. Humans could be very fragile at times.

"Can I help you?" Miles asked. It was less a question of whether he could actually help Taryn, but more a matter of whether she would let him help her. One could never be too careful in cross-species relationships such as this one, especially in the first encounter.

"I don't know if I can walk," Taryn said.

"That's all right," Miles answered. "I was planning to carry you."

Taryn screamed as Miles reached down with long and strong arms and scooped her up. But it only took a moment before she realized what had happened. Miles had not intended to hurt her. He had not hurt her at all. But he had managed to pick her and her backpack up without so much as a grunt of effort. And a moment later, Taryn looked around to find herself almost hurtling through the trees. But she was not flying. She was still safe within the arms of Bigfoot as he swiftly carried her away from the site of her injury.

"Where are you taking me?" Taryn asked, her voice shaky. This was definitely not what she had expected when she finally found a sign of the elusive Bigfoot. She figured she might find a footprint or a bit of fur or hair stuck to a tree. If she was really lucky, she might come across some sort of nest that a Bigfoot might use to sleep in. She never expected to actually find the creature itself.

"I know someplace you will be much more comfortable," Miles said.

Taryn nodded her head into Bigfoot's chest, for once thankful she did not need to solely rely on herself to get her out of her situation. She had someone helping her. Although getting help from the very creature she had been searching for was seriously unexpected.

"You can speak English," Taryn said, unable to stop herself from voicing her curiosity. "How?"

"I pick up things here and there," Miles said. "I get bored sometimes and like to stalk hikers. Listening to them I've learned a lot. And I've managed to collect a few books over time and have even taught myself how to read."

He seemed so matter of fact about it, as if learning to speak and read were simple feats. But everything Taryn had learned about more primitive species of hominids or whatever Miles really was, that should not have been possible. And yet, there he was, both speaking and supposedly reading. And to do it on his own was even more impressive.

"Wait," Taryn said, suddenly realizing something. "Were you stalking me?"

"No, no, no," Miles said. "I heard you scream when you fell and I came to investigate. I wouldn't have even gotten close, but I saw you were hurt. I just wanted to help."

Taryn was not sure if she could trust that answer, but she did not see herself having much choice. Without Miles helping her, she would have a very difficult time returning home.

It was impossible for Taryn to determine how far Miles carried her. He could move so much faster through the forest than she could have. Between his long legs eating up the ground and his intimate familiarity with the terrain, Taryn had little doubt he could travel a mile in mere minutes. That was much faster than whatever she could manage as she pushed her way through the dense foliage.

But when Miles finally did stop, he did so after entering a clearing alongside a cliff face. There was a cave, but it wasn't dark and scary. There were lights inside. I didn't understand. Had Miles somehow managed to obtain electric lights somehow? He had learned to speak and read. What else had he done?

Miles took her inside and set me down on a woven mat. There were several mats spread out around the cave entrance area. There was a narrow passage, but it looked like there was more space deeper in the cave, an actual chamber or something like that. Taryn was no expert on caves. She had always assumed Bigfoot either created a wooded nest for itself or even lived in the trees. She had not seriously considered caves as a living space. Looking back, it was a major oversight.

"How?" was all Taryn could ask as she looked around the cave. The lights were actually flowers that fluoresced. They produced their own light, thus lighting the cave and making it more habitable. But Taryn had never heard of plants that could produce such light. She did not think such things existed.

"Do you mean the flowers or how I learned to speak?" Miles asked as he busied himself in what looked like a part of a hollowed out log.

"The flowers, but really, both," Taryn answered.

Miles continued digging through the log as if it was a trunk or other container. He was looking for something. Whatever it was, he had quite a setup. And Taryn could only assume he had done all of this himself. Unless there were others like him.

"I learned how to graft plants from my mother," Miles explained. "She taught me almost everything I know for survival. But I was the one who discovered how to create plants that glow like this and produce light. As for speaking, I found a radio that a hiker dropped once and that got me started on learning language. I later found a guidebook and taught myself how to read from that. You humans leave a lot of stuff behind."

Taryn sat there stunned. She certainly could not argue with him about how much trash humans produced and how it found its way into so many places that it should not have. But it was also perfectly clear that Miles, a Bigfoot or Sasquatch or whatever other name he wanted to call his species, was not just some big hairy ape. He was intelligent in ways that completely defied logic.

It was only now that Taryn could take in Miles in his

entirety. He was large, far taller than she was. He sported a reddish-brown coat of hair that almost entirely covered his body. Only his face was partially clear of hair, but his protruding mouth looked very ape-like, or at least a bit like Homer Simpson. And yet, there was an intelligence in his eyes that she could not have ever guessed would have been there.

"Just so you know," Taryn said. "I was out here looking for you."

Miles stopped what he was doing and turned and looked at her. He studied her for a moment, trying to assess her intentions. He normally never would have interfered in her business, but he had seen her fall and heard her cries of pain. He had already decided to trust her with his secret. The only question was whether she was actually trustworthy of it. He would hate to have to pack up his cave and find a new one to live in. He had already done that before and he was not eager to do it again.

"I had a feeling," Miles said. "It's not often someone finds their way off the beaten trail around these parts. It's one reason I live where I do. I am a solitary creature. I generally prefer my privacy."

"And yet you decided to help me," Taryn said.

"I'm not a monster, even if people might think I look like one."

"I don't think you're a monster. You've been kind to me. I don't know what I'd do without your help."

Miles returned to rummaging through the trunk. "Oh, there it is." He pulled out something bundled in something similar to the woven mat Taryn sat on. The mat was a bit on the crude side, but it kept her from sitting in the dirt or on the hard rock. The material was definitely plant based, largely unprocessed, simply picked and woven before it had a chance to completely dry out.

"What is that?" Taryn asked as Miles unwrapped the object in his hands.

"There's an old family recipe for a healing drink my mother passed along to me. These are dried leaves from a very rare plant. By making a tea, I should have you back on your feet in a day or so."

"Wow, that's amazing," Taryn said, surprised both by the claim made, but also Miles' generosity. This was another sign that Miles was far smarter than anyone she had ever met. Humans did not have teas that could cure possibly broken bones in a day.

"Just let me work my magic and we'll see what I can do."

Miles busied himself making a pot of tea with the special leaves for Taryn. As he did his work, Taryn focused on getting her boot off so that she could better see the damage to her ankle and foot. Removing the boot relieved some of the pain, but only because it had started to swell. Taryn did not know if it was broken or not, but there was no way she would be walking out of the forest on her own.

It took nearly half an hour before Miles had finished making Taryn's tea. He even had little wooden cups to drink from. They had been blocks of wood that had been carved out. How Miles had been able to do all of this remained a mystery, but he was no doubt resourceful. And talented.

"Thank you," Taryn said as she accepted the cup of tea. She brought the steaming liquid up to her lips and took a deep breath, pulling the steam up into her nose, smelling the liquid for the first time. It smelled decent, although Taryn had never been a tea drinker. Her preference usually came in the form of hot chocolate.

But the moment Taryn took her first sip, she found herself unable to stop drinking the almost sweet tea. She slurped it down, ignoring the heat as it nearly burned her mouth and throat. It collected in her stomach and sent warm tendrils of comfort around her body.

The pain in Taryn's foot and ankle began to dissipate almost immediately. The throbbing slowed. Taryn smiled. It was not just her foot that felt better. Her head felt light and happy.

"It's okay if you fall asleep," Miles offered. He pulled out a woven blanket. The blanket was more finely woven and lacked the stiffness of the mats. He spread it over Taryn's body as she drifted off to sleep, lulled there by the comforting tea.

When Taryn woke up she struggled to remember what had happened. Her thoughts came to her slowly, as if she was drunk or high, but she did not feel like she was either. She felt completely sober.

"My ankle," Taryn said out loud, remembering her injury. She pulled off the blanket that covered her and looked down at her foot and ankle. The swelling was gone. Her ankle looked completely healed. It was a miracle. She had never seen someone heal that fast before. Whatever that family recipe was, it was ingenious.

However, it did not take long before Taryn's gaze drifted elsewhere. She looked down and was greeted by an unexpected sight. Between her eyes and her ankle stood two mounds. They were where her breasts were supposed to be, but Taryn had never been a big woman when it came to her bust. She had always been slim all over and what she did have was often minimized with a sports bra. But what she saw were whompers. They were big and round and completely foreign to her.

"What happened?" Taryn asked quizzically. However, as soon as those words were spoken, she slapped her hand across her mouth, shocked at the sound of her voice. The pitch was significantly higher than she remembered it being. It was hard to think, what with her mind still sluggish from whatever was in the tea, but she was certain her voice was higher pitched.

But as Taryn touched her mouth, she became much more aware of how much her lips had plumped up. They were soft and plush. It was actually impressive that her lips had not caused her to lisp. They were that big.

Taryn climbed to her feet, trying to get a better idea of what had happened to her. She still had her boot on her good foot, although she no longer seemed to have an injured foot. Both feet could completely hold her weight. Her center of gravity definitely felt off. Her large bust pulled her forward. At this size, they were definitely tits, although there still seemed to be a disconnect in her head about that.

But as Taryn checked herself out, she noticed her butt had expanded as well. It filled out her shorts completely, making them look almost painted on. Yet as scary as the physical changes should have been for Taryn, she felt no panic or even concern. The fact was, every change she had experienced thus far left her feeling good. They made her feel pretty.

Feeling pretty had never been particularly important to Taryn before. She knew she looked decent enough. But it was not as if the National Park ranger uniform was exactly form fitting or flattering. And that was how she dressed most of the time. Even her personal clothing collection was similar to what she wore while working.

Now, however, it felt different. Taryn could not understand why, but her appearance seemed far more important to her than it ever had before. She wanted to look pretty first and foremost. Maybe it had something to do with the tingle she felt deep in her belly. It was not exactly familiar, but she recognized it as arousal. She was getting horny.

"Oh good, you're awake," Miles said as he stepped through the narrow gap in the back of the cave. Presumably beyond that opening was his bedroom.

But as soon as Miles was able to rise to his full height and looked at Taryn straight on, he paused, unable to fully comprehend what had happened. The woman he saw before him only had a passing resemblance to the woman he had saved the day before. She looked like an over-sexualized caricature of her former self.

"Hi, Miles," Taryn said with a chipper attitude. She smiled at him as she bounced up and down on the balls of her feet. That, in turn, made her big tits bounce and jiggle under her now tight top.

"Well, I'll be," Miles said as he fully comprehended what had just happened. "My mother warned me about using her recipes with other species. Now I understand why."

"I don't get it," Taryn said as she started to twirl a lock of hair with her finger. She stood there with a confused look on her face, slowly coming to terms with the new normal of her reality. This was who she was now. Her past life as a National Park ranger and as an avid Bigfoot hunter was over. She was now nothing more than a sexy bimbo who needed to use her body to get by, because her mind was simply no longer able to handle complicated matters.

Miles buried his face in his hands, shaking his head at the mistake he had made. Yes, her foot and ankle were healed, looking better than ever. But everything else about Taryn had changed. The tea had turned her into a bimbo. Yes, she was made for a sexy bimbo, but it was still a radical change from her past self. And it was all Miles' fault.

"Okay, get your boot on," Miles said with a sigh. He had not expected to play babysitter to a bimbo, but as sexy as she was, Taryn was not his type. Besides, even her bimbofied body was unlikely able to handle him when he was fully aroused. For that, he would need a female Bigfoot. He might find his partner someday, but with all of his species living in relative isolation, it was difficult to find romantic partners. "I'm taking you back to the trail so you can find your way home."

"But I'm horny," Taryn said, pouting petulantly. Taryn was not the kind of person anymore to care whether she fucked Bigfoot or a human male. She just wanted to fuck. She just needed to answer the call of her bimbofied body.

"Nope," Miles said. "I'm not even considering it. You can find a man when you get back to the trailhead. I presume your car is there somewhere. Once you get back to the trail, you're on your own. I'm sorry that I ever helped you."

Miles considered walking Taryn back to the trail, but he ended up carrying her. It was just easier that way and she was less likely to get distracted. She seemed to have the attention span of a gnat now. All it took was to spot something shiny or pretty and she completely forgot about the last thing she had just been talking about. Miles doubted she had many thoughts that were not vocalized. Her IQ had caved into the double digits. How far it had fallen would be difficult to measure. She no longer had the attention span to take such a test.

Taryn did enjoy getting carried by Miles. She enjoyed him holding her nubile body against his strong and hair one. He was all corded muscle, but his thick hair made him soft. And his natural wild odor was growing on her.

As Miles carried Taryn back to the trail, he did realize no one would believe her if she blabbed about him. That was a benefit to what had happened. He would be safe to continue living in his cave. And even if she did manage to tell someone about him, and get them to believe her, there was no way she would be able to lead them back to him or his cave. There was nothing to worry about.

"You were really nice to me, Miles," Taryn said when he finally set her down. Her feet were on the trail, although she had no idea which way she should go.

Miles pointed the direction he wanted her to go. It would take her down toward the trailhead where she had parked her car. Taryn blew Miles a kiss with her plump lips before she turned and started skipping down the trail in the direction he had pointed.

There was a part of Miles that felt bad about what had happened. However, he knew it had probably all been for the best. He only hoped Taryn would be happy in her new life as a bimbo. She at least seemed to be happy, even if she had pouted over Miles not taking advantage of her. Then again, she had no way of knowing that she was about as far from Miles' type as could be. Her nearly hairless body simply did nothing for the Bigfoot. He recognized her sexiness by human standards, but human standards were very different from Bigfoot standards.

Taryn skipped down the trail, loving the feel of her bouncing tits. They made her feel so sexy and feeling sexy made her feel horny. But in one of the few thoughts that managed to make it through her molasses filled mind, she decided she liked being horny. It felt good. It made her feel alive and present in her own body. And the more present she felt in her body, the less she had to think. She definitely wanted to avoid thinking as much as possible. Too many thoughts would hurt her head or make her sad.

With no idea where she was going or what she was going to do, Taryn just continued down the trail. It was the offseason, so there was not a high chance she would meet another hiker. And before she knew it, she had reached her car.

It took Taryn a moment to figure out how to unlock it. The car was old and the key fob no longer worked.

"Key in lock like cock in pussy," Taryn said to herself, giggling the whole time at her sex joke. But it was necessary for her to focus enough to get the key into the lock so she could open her car.

Taryn's first order of business was not driving away, but was instead changing her clothes. For one, her fall had left her clothes in a gross state, There was mud everywhere. At some point she would need a shower or a nice hot bath, but in the meantime, she just needed to change into other clothes. But with the bimbofication of her mind and body, Taryn also wanted better looking clothes. She wanted to look like the sexy bimbo she had become.

The trunk was filled with various items. There was nothing

really valuable there, just clothes and a few supplies she had left behind. However, among the clothing was a green bikini. Taryn's original plan for the bikini was in case she needed to stay over at a motel and they had a hot tub for a post expedition soak. But that was before Taryn's mind and body had changed. A bikini made sense for swimwear then. Now it made sense for regular clothing.

The trailhead was deserted, but even if there had been other people, the new Taryn would have had no qualms in changing in front of people. It might even lead to sex. Sure, there might be an angry girlfriend or wife, but Taryn could not be bothered with checking whether a guy was with someone before she let him fuck her. Besides, the other woman should have been sexier if she wanted to keep her man from straying.

"Much better," Taryn said to herself as she stood there in her bikini. She tossed her old clothes and her pack into the trunk and then sashayed around the car toward the driver door. She did not need to swing her hips like that. There was no one to show off to, but it was good practice. And besides, if there was someone hiding in the woods, she wanted to make sure their eyes were where she wanted them. She wanted them to look at her and make her their sole focus of attention.

Once behind the wheel of her car, Taryn could not be bothered with the thought of driving home. That was far too long for her to focus. Instead, as soon as she made it down to the closest town, she started looking for how she wanted to spend the rest of her day. As a horny bimbo, sex was at the forefront of her mind.

And then she saw it. It was called the Hideaway. And the neon signs made it clear what kind of establishment it was. Where before Taryn had been interested in biology, ecology, geology and even archeology, now she was mostly interested in sex. It was about all her bimbofied brain could handle now that she was perpetually horny. And Taryn had no doubt that a strip club would be the perfect place for her. She could dance for all those men, turning them on with her body, and if she was lucky, she could get someone to fuck her afterward. That seemed like the best of all possibilities.

Taryn parked her car outside the Hideaway and strode in with a sexy wiggle. She was pretty sure she would fit right in wearing her bikini. It might even take people a little while to realize she was not one of the strippers already.

The wolf whistle from the bar was the first thing Taryn heard. It was still early in the day and there were only a handful of customers. The music was relatively mild with one stripped on stage, milking the early crowd for every dollar they could spare. This was not a high class strip club, but that suited Taryn just fine. She was not a high class bimbo.

Taryn looked over at the bar. In addition to the bartender, a big burly looking man who stood there cleaning a glass with a rag, there was also a man sitting there pouring over a notebook. He looked like the manager or the owner. He was also the man who had whistled at her.

Taryn headed straight for the man, giggling at his whistling compliment. There had been a time when Taryn would have scowled and possibly even slapped a man who wolf whistled her, but that was before she became a bimbo. That was before her sole goal in life was to be as sexy as possible. That was before all she really wanted was a steady stream of men to fuck.

"I'm guessing you want a job," the man said.

Taryn bit her lip and nodded her head.

"Well, let me see what you've got," the man said. "Show me your body."

Taryn stood up straight and thrust out her impressive chest. That right there would have been enough to get her hired. But she did a slow turn, making sure to show off everything she had to her future employer. And Taryn was not just a bimbo with a great rack. She had a tight midriff and a well-developed ass. She was the whole package.

"Oh yeah," the man said. "There's just one thing I need from you before I can hire you. Come with me into the back."

Taryn, who had not even given the man her name yet, followed him into the back, toward his office. Once there, Taryn felt the overwhelming need to kneel before him. She dropped to her knees without a second's hesitation, bringing her lips level with the growing bulge in the man's pants.

"You knew what I was thinking," the man said. "Good girl."

Taryn quivered as a shot of pleasure shot through her body. She loved being called a good girl. But that was short lived, as soon the man had his cock out. He was big, but that did not stop Taryn. She took him into her mouth, wrapping her plump lips around his cock and giving him the best blowjob she could manage, including taking him deep into her throat, just like a good bimbo should. The fact that Taryn had never given a blowjob before in her life never crossed her mind. Nothing crossed her mind except the determination to make her new boss cum in her mouth.

"Damn," the man said as he came hard in Taryn's mouth. She was so good that his usual stamina failed him. "You are one talented cocksucker."

Taryn beamed up at him, enjoying the compliment. She might not be smart anymore, but she could certainly use her body to best effect. She could suck cock, she could fuck cock, she could even take a cock up her ass or get it off with her tits. Nothing was beyond her. When it came to sex, Taryn was the total package.

"You're hired," the man said as Taryn continued to kneel before him, his cock still hanging in front of her eyes. She was still horny and knew that cock was the answer. She needed to get fucked.

"Thank you so much," Taryn finally said as she looked up at her new boss.

"Now go get yourself cleaned up," the man said. "There's a shower in the dressing room, along with outfits and makeup. Shoes too. You're on in an hour. If you do a good job in your first set, I'll make sure you get fucked."

Taryn almost wondered how he knew what she really wanted. Almost. Instead, she jumped up and hurried toward the dressing room. The back of the club was relatively simple with several VIP rooms, the manager's office, and the dressing room. Even. A bimbo could find her way around.

It took the whole hour for Taryn to ready herself. She showered and then applied a load of makeup that she had never used before, but managed to figure it out. When it came time to choose an outfit, she really liked her green bikini. It reminded her of the forest where her bimbo life began. It reminded her of Miles. She managed to find some other costume pieces that fit with her forest theme, fans and headpieces that included big green leaves and other forest related accessories.

When Taryn stepped out on stage, the music was playing and the DJ announced her as Bambi, which made no sense to her, but as a bimbo, she was not going to argue about it. And maybe she really was Bambi. Taryn did not sound like a good bimbo name, but Bambi did. Little did the newly minted Bambi realize that her name meant child of the forest. It was a perfect fit.

Bambi danced on stage to impressive hoots and hollers from the growing crowd. Money kept getting deposited on stage as Bambi danced, slowly removing her costume until she finished the song wearing only a pair of green stripper heels. Her set ended with further cheers as she picked up her costume and all her money.

As soon as she was backstage, the owner stopped her, placing a hand on her shoulder.

"Good job out there, Bambi," the man said, using her stage name. By this point, she had fully internalized her new name, pushing out her remaining memories of ever being called Taryn. She was just Bambi now. She was Bambi the bimbo stripper. "I think you deserve a reward."

Before Bambi knew what was happening, she had returned to the manager's office. Her cash and costume had been deposited on a chair. She was bent over the desk, her boss pounding her from behind. He told her the room was sound proofed. It was a good thing too, because Bambi turned out to be quite the screamer when it came to sex. And when it was all done, Bambi could only smile. The orgasm had been better than anything she had ever felt before. She loved her new name, her new job, her new life. It was perfect for a bimbo like her.

Bambi's boss took care of everything for her, making her old life disappear. He set her up in a little apartment next to the club. He owned both buildings, so it was an easy setup for him. And Bambi did not even need to pay rent. As long as she kept fucking him whenever he wanted, he was happy to keep her around. And once word got around about her, the club patronage saw a big boost. It was a small town, but people drove in from all over to see Bambi dance. And for those who were willing to pay extra, they got a lot more than that in the VIP rooms. No one ever told Bambi she could not fuck the customers, but no one seemed to mind. Even the police chief got in on the action, becoming one of her regulars.

As far as Bambi could think, she had the best life possible. She did not miss being Taryn at all. She was just Bambi now and her life revolved around the club. Even if her boss had specified that she was to take days off, she would still end up at the club. It was where she wanted to spend all her time. Bambi kept her forest themed costumes. It just felt right.

Her boss made Taryn disappear. Her car was hauled off and dumped deep in the forest, miles away. No one would suspect that Bambi had once been the former National Park ranger. There was even a note left in the car for searchers to find, with Taryn promising to live in the woods and give up civilized life. Once that was found, the search for her was called off. Bambi was safe to be the bimbo stripper slut she now wanted to be without interference from anyone else. It was a perfect life for her. It was the life she wanted to live.

However, Bambi always kept an eye out for a tall creature with lots of reddish brown hair. She kept an eye out for Miles, just in case he ever snuck into town to check up on her. She had no idea where he was or what he was doing. But there was a part of her that still wanted to fuck him. It was the one thing that would make her life truly complete, the opportunity to fuck Miles and his Bigfoot cock.

BIMBO ZERO

"The B-Virus has breached containment," Beck said. He had a worried look on his face.

Alice's heart hammered in her chest at the news. Could it be true? Had their creation really broken containment? Was the B-Virus out in the wild?

"Are you sure?" Alice said, still hopeful that her life's work had not blown up in her face. Despite all the people who worked on the virus in the lab, studying its effects on human tissue, the research had been her baby and she ultimately felt responsible for whatever happened with it.

"Look," Beck said, pointing out the window. It was obvious, the signs clear.

A woman stood outside the window. Her clothes were barely able to contain her curves, not because she had such substantial curves, which she did, but because her clothing had never been designed to contain such curves. Her body had practically exploded, her breasts and butt growing to large proportions.

But it was not her body that so specifically made it clear she had been infected with the B-Virus. The woman's body could have been created through other means and she could have dressed herself in clothing that wanted to rip apart at the seams. Some people were into that sort of thing. No, it was the vacant, glassy-eyed stare that made it clear what had happened. And it meant the B-Virus was affecting people outside of the lab, people who had never stepped foot inside the research areas.

"This is bad," Alice said, having just come in from outside herself.

The B-Virus was supposed to be a safe virus to research. It had strange ways of spreading and usually required direct contact. As long as the research scientists Alice and Beck oversaw maintained their anti-exposure protocols, everything would have been fine. But clearly something had happened. The virus had somehow escaped the lab and now it could spread unimpeded by the safety protocols Alice had put in place to prevent just such an event.

Alice immediately pulled out her phone. This was a call she had never wanted to make before. When she first got hired at the research laboratory, she had programmed a series of phone numbers into her phone. Her reason was to always be ready should something at the lab breach containment. Her finger was already moving toward the call button.

"Wait," Beck said. "Maybe there's still time for us to fix this. You know as well as I do that some of our research wasn't authorized."

Alice paused, knowing Beck was telling the truth. In fact, the B-Virus research, while supposed to be safe, had already been banned by the federal government. But the discovery of the B-Virus was like Pandora's Box. It could not be taken back. Once it was known, it was only inevitable that it would attract people interested in researching it.

It had been easy enough to obtain a sample on the black market. From there, the virus was easy to replicate, making sure they would always have an adequate supply. The government never needed to know that they had broken the law. That was, until now. However, Alice had already crossed the ethical line of partaking in illegal research. If there was a chance to avoid jail time, the only way to do it was to keep the feds out of their business. They had to deal with this themselves.

"Okay, you're right," Alice said. "Now let's go. We need to get the woman off the street and into the lab."

Alice and Beck acted swiftly. The woman had yet to move when security, dressed in full hazmat suits, approached her. They found it easy to guide her into the lab. She went with them willingly, unable to argue with their obvious logic. They did not even need to make false promises to her.

The B-Virus did one thing. It turned women into bimbos. When the virus had first been discovered, its effects were considered to take a long time, transforming the woman into a bimbo over weeks, if not months. But as Alice, Beck, and the rest of the lab started their research, a new variant emerged. This variant was significantly faster. It only took minutes for the women to transform now. The whole process could take less than an hour.

And what was more, the new variant was considerably stronger than the original. The body modifications were more severe, resulting in larger breasts, a larger butt, plumper lips, and all the rest. The mental effects were stronger too. What started as a basic memory suppressant and libido booster now turned the woman into a bit of a zombie. The infected women would just stand there, staring at nothing until something grabbed her attention. Usually that required a man or the promise of some sort of sex.

In the case of the infected woman outside the lab, all the security team had to do was place a hand on her ass and guide her off the street. She went willingly, although it was pretty clear she only had one thing on her mind. She was horny and desired sex. Nothing else mattered. She was so easily compliant, because she understood going with the security team, even dressed as they were, could lead to sex. It was that simple.

As soon as the infected woman had been brought in off the street, Alice tried to figure out who she was.

"Ma'am," Alice said, still wearing the hazmat suit. She did not want to get infected herself. That would be a disaster. She did not want to be a bimbo. "Can you tell me your name?"

The woman briefly looked toward Alice, but she showed no sign of understanding what Alice had asked. Instead, she just giggled. And once she started giggling, there was nothing anyone could do to stop her, except from giving her something new to attract her attention. But she was so far gone the only way to stop her from giggling would have been for one of the men to pull out his cock and show it to her. Not that any of the men were willing to do that. They all knew it would lead to getting fired.

"Check her purse," Alice finally said, realizing she was not going to get anything out of the infected woman. She was too far gone. The B-Virus did not just turn people into bimbos, it almost made them into sex-obsessed zombies. Or at least that was what the research indicated. However, the behavior of this woman made that reasonably clear. She responded to men, but not to women. And the way she licked her lips and looked reverently toward anyone she recognized as male made it more obvious.

Of course, the B-Virus did not seem to have any effect on men. There was something about the male chromosomes that fully repelled the B-Virus entirely. They could not even carry it. Luckily, it appeared that infection did not last long in women. A few hours after transforming, they were free of the virus. Alice's only hope was that any break of containment burned itself out quickly. For all Alice knew, this woman was the only person infected. And in a few more hours, everything would be fine and back to normal.

And even better, the company that funded Alice and Beck's research had deep enough pockets and had always been willing to operate within the gray area when it came to moral and ethical behavior, the woman was certain to be well taken care of. The company PR people would find a way to spin the woman's transformation without it causing suspicion.

"Her driver's license says her name is Jennifer Davis," one of the security guards said. "We can run a background check on her to figure out what kind of trouble she might cause us."

"Call me Jenni," the woman suddenly said after hearing her name. Although it seemed to almost be an involuntary response.

There was no signal that she understood who she was or what had happened to her. She just existed now.

"Okay, Jenni," Beck said, taking charge of the situation. "Let's get you situated. Follow me and I'll take you to your room."

They did not have rooms set up for patients, but there were bedrooms at the lab. They were routinely checked out by staff when their work required them to remain at the lab for long periods of time. It was easier to keep tabs on an experiment when naps could be taken in a nearby room than to require the researcher to drive back and forth between work and their home so that they could fit in an hour of sleep here and there. And it was clear much of the staff would be using those rooms until the potential containment breach had been resolved.

As soon as Beck left with Jenni, Alice returned to her office. Once alone, she pulled off her hazmat gear. As far as she knew, she was safe. She always found the hazmat suits to be hot and confining. It did not help that she was looking at having to wear it a lot more until the outbreak was resolved. Anytime she was in a situation where she could be exposed, she would need to wear it. The men might have been able to get away without it, but none of the women at the lab were so lucky.

Alice took several deep breaths, enjoying her freedom from the hazmat suit. Her body was tired, a result of the adrenaline boost she got from seeing Jenni. The knowledge that her research project was out in the wild scared the hell out of her. As much as she had done everything right, she was certain the company executives would find a way to blame her if knowledge of the B-Virus escaping became public.

Of course, Alice knew there were some men who would welcome the B-Virus running rampant through the world's population. To Alice, those men were sexist pigs and did not deserve to breathe the same air as she did. They were gross and she hoped the world would move on from them completely, stamping out their existence as women continued to make improvements in their lives and to the world as a whole.

Alice looked back outside. She had been standing here moments earlier when Jenni had first been spotted. There was no one there now. The street was empty. But the fact Jenni had contracted the B-Virus made it clear that something bad had happened.

Suddenly the phone rang. It was her office phone and not her cell phone.

"This is Dr. Terrapin," she said, answering the phone. She tried not to let her worry creep into her voice. She knew she needed to sound confident and in charge.

"It's Rose," came the familiar voice on the line. She was one of the researchers on the B-Virus project. "Dr. Sinclair just told me another infected woman has been discovered."

Alice's jaw dropped open. There was another one? It did not seem possible. And how had Beck found out about it while he was dealing with Jenni? It did not make sense. But if anyone was going to know more than her, it was Dr. Beck Sinclair. He was her right hand man in the research of the B-Virus. If he said something, she trusted him that it would be true.

"Do you have an address?" Alice asked.

"Yes, Dr. Sinclair gave it to me," Rose answered.

"All right, we're going to go deal with this. Bring your hazmat suit. We're going on a field trip."

It was only a few minutes before Alice and Rose found themselves in a black company SUV on their way to a suspected second B-Virus case. It was apparently far enough away where they needed to drive. That was not good as far as containment went. Not that they knew how the B-Virus was spreading. Their research had been difficult to ascertain that information without purposefully infecting people. They might have operated in a gray zone, but that was too far, even for them.

Rose sat behind the wheel, driving. She knew the address.

Alice rode shotgun. They wore their hazmat suits, but left their helmets off. Wearing them would have made driving difficult. Plus, they were pretty sure neither of them were contagious. The chance of spread was almost zero.

But as soon as Rose pulled over to the side of the street, parking along the curb, Alice knew something was wrong.

"What?" Rose asked, seeing the worried expression on her boss' face.

"This is my neighbor's house," Alice said. "My house is right back there."

It was true. Had Rose shared the address before they got in the car, Alice would have behaved differently on the drive over. She might not even have gone at all. Something strange was going on. The problem was Alice could not understand it. She was worried about trying to chase down the containment breach, stopping the spread of a bimbofying virus. But she was beginning to wonder if something else was going on. She just did not know what it could be.

"Put your helmet on," Alice ordered. "I may need your help in collecting Diana. She's my neighbor and if she's been infected, there's no telling who else could be."

Fully protected with their hazmat helmets on, the pair walked up the front walk of Alice's neighbor's house. She had known her neighbor ever since she moved in. Diana was a nice woman, if not a little strange at times. Alice had always thought of her neighbor as a hippie. Her yard was wild with plants. They were all well cared for, but the yard always looked overgrown.

Alice looked over to see her own house standing there. It did not make sense how the virus could have spread here unless Diana had been near the lab. Alice was disappointed she would not be able to stop at home. As soon as they found Diana, they needed to bring her into the lab for further testing. Although if what Beck had said was true, Diana had already transformed and was probably no longer contagious.

"Make sure your air supply is turned on," Alice said, warning Rose, just in case. The last thing they needed was a surprise.

"I'm good," Rose said. She sounded more calm than Alice did. Then again, Rose might not fully understand what the B-Virus could do to a woman. She had not seen Jenni.

Alice led the way up onto the porch. Then she reached out and rang the doorbell. There was no telling what would happen next. Would Diana answer the door? If she were fully transformed, she might not respond at all. It was impossible to know. Technically, Alice had a key, just in case. The neighbors had exchanged keys early on, just in case one or the other got locked out or there was an emergency while one of them was away. Neither of them had any pets, so at least that would not be an issue.

Alice could hear the doorbell ring on the other side of the door. It was loud enough to wake the dead. Hopefully that would entice Diana to come to the door if she was infected. She certainly would if she was her normal self.

Despite wearing her helmet, Alice could still see into the house a little bit. The front door had a large window in it, although the glare of both the glass and the clear plastic cover on her helmet made it difficult to get a good view. But there was movement. That much Alice was certain of. Someone was inside.

It took a few moments, but the door finally started to open. Alice gave a sigh of relief, believing that meant Diana was fine, that this had been a false alarm. But the moment the door opened fully, giving Alice a view of her neighbor, she knew all hope had been lost. Diana had been a petite woman, but that was over and done with. Her body had been massively transformed. Her chest was massive, her butt equally big, her lips barely able to open to make sound. There was no doubt that she had been infected.

Jenni had clearly had the worst of it as far as mental side

effects went. She had practically turned into a zombie. Diana, on the other hand, still seemed to retain a little of the intelligent spark that she had once had fully. It was significantly dulled, but it was still there, barely.

"Hi," Diana said. "My name's Didi."

Alice inwardly groaned at hearing her once intelligent neighbor sound like a complete airhead. Diana had once been smart. She was a writer, specializing in technical writing. Alice had forgotten the company her neighbor worked for, but it had been a big one making computer chips or something like that. But that Diana was gone. She had been replaced by Didi, a bimbo.

"Diana, I'm your neighbor, Alice. Do you remember who I am?"

"Oh, hi, Alice," Didi said. "I didn't, you know, recognize you and stuff with that funny suit you're wearing. And you should call me Didi. That's a much funner name."

"Okay, Didi," Alice said. "I'm glad you remember who I am. This is my coworker, Rose. We need to take you to the lab I work at. We have reason to believe you've been infected by a virus."

"Well," Didi started to say. She was clearly torn. "I invited the pizza boy over for some fun. He's really cute."

"If we go now, you might be able to get back in time to meet with him," Rose said.

Alice looked over at her coworker and was impressed by the logic Rose had just used. Yes, that was the way to persuade a bimbo to do what they wanted.

"And there are lots of men at the lab," Alice added.

"I like men," Didi said before she broke out into a fit of giggles. "Do you know why? It's because they have cocks."

"Yes, yes," Alice said. "Now come with us and we'll make sure you get all the cock you need."

Didi showed no hesitation or trepidation at being led away

from her house. She was easily persuadable when it came to things like men.

The street was empty, making the trip back even easier. First, there was no one out when they led Didi down the front path and loaded her into the back of the SUV. Then it was a quick trip back to the lab itself. Before they knew it, they had Didi loaded into one of the extra rooms at the lab. It was done.

However, the whole way Alice found herself wondering how Didi had been exposed to the B-Virus. It was clear to anyone with any knowledge about the virus what had happened. The only question was how it had happened.

"Am I the vector?" Alice asked herself as she drove back to the lab.

"What was that?" Rose asked from the passenger seat. They had switched jobs for the drive back. But this time they had kept the hazmat helmets on, not wanting to risk infection from Didi, just in case she still had the virus circulating in her system. They both doubted it based on how lucid Didi not seemed. She was still very much a bimbo, but she seemed less zombie-like than Jenni had.

"Nothing," Alice said. "I was just talking to myself."

The truth was, Alice was going through her mind, trying to think about what interactions she had with Diana recently. Their schedules rarely lined up. Alice was the type of person to work late and come into the office a little later than most people. In comparison, Diana had always been an early riser. However, Alice suddenly remembered running into Diana as they both grabbed the mail from the mailboxes on the street. Their mailboxes were only a foot or so apart. It meant they were briefly in close proximity to each other. But that should not have been enough for transmission, especially since Alice had been infected. The breach had not happened until today.

Alice shook her head, not believing it was possible. There had to be another explanation. That was all there was to it. The breach had been today. That's when they saw the virus do its thing. Not that Didi would be able to fill them in on her travels earlier in the day. She was too much of a bimbo for that. But maybe Beck might be able to reason with her better and get additional answers out of her. The bimbos definitely responded differently to men than they did women. It had to be a sex thing.

"You were right about the spread," Alice told Beck the next time they saw each other. Didi had been placed in a room in the lab with Jenni. It was obvious they had both contracted the B-Virus. Their symptoms were unique to this particular virus. But that did not explain how the virus had breached containment.

"I almost always am," Beck said. He seemed cockier than usual, beyond confident.

There had been a time when Alice might have considered Beck as a romantic partner, but after years spent together in the lab, those chances were long since past. As far as Alice knew, they had both moved on with their lives. Not that either of them had much luck in the romance department. The long hours tended to do that, making dating difficult. But the benefits included the chance to be on the cutting edge of virology research. That seemed reasonable in Alice's mind.

The pair sat back in Alice's office. They each needed a break. The hazmat suits had come off and Alice had put her feet up on her desk, sitting back and taking a breather. Beck sat across from her. Even though his feet were planted on the floor, he still had a casual air about him. Although he kept looking at Alice as if he expected something to happen. But Alice did not notice anything untoward. She was just tired after picking up Didi.

Her mind raced as she tried to figure out the path of the virus. Unfortunately, the bimbofied women provided poor information when it came to their recent activities and movements. They fully cooperated with the questions asked of them, there was no deceit or subterfuge, but the information that remained in the brains seemed impossible to access. The women could not describe what they had been doing moments earlier, let alone what they had been doing over the course of the past 24 hours.

"So we have two infected people with no known connection to the lab," Alice said, trying to go over the information they had collected for what felt like the fifth time. No matter how much she wanted to completely take a break and relax, her mind was still fixated on the problem they faced. There was no other way forward until they solved the breach.

"Jenni was found outside the lab, so that is tangentially connected," Beck said as a reminder.

"True. And we caught her right after it happened, so her exposure was still fresh. It happened today."

Beck nodded his head in agreement. There was nothing more he needed to add.

"So it means she could have come into inadvertent contact with almost anyone from the lab," Alice continued, working the problem out loud. "But there's no guarantee that she even was a close contact to someone who works here. She could have picked it up elsewhere and it just happened to be a coincidence that she was outside this office when her transformation took place."

"It's Didi that has you most worried, isn't it?" Beck asked. They had both started using her preferred name, although Alice still thought of her neighbor as Diana in her head.

"Yes," Alice said, nodding absentmindedly. "I don't know how she could have gotten it. If I had been infected, then I would have already transformed. It means she couldn't have gotten it from me. Someone else either ran into her somewhere or she was specifically targeted."

"You really think someone is targeting people you know?" Beck asked. It was a simple question, but one with far reaching implications. If there was someone targeting her, it meant there was someone stalking her.

"I can't believe that," Alice answered. "I can't rule it out, but I can't believe it either. Yes, my role in the B-Virus research is significant, but in the big picture, I'm a minor player."

This time it was Beck nodding his head, agreeing that Alice's role in the research was limited. Yes, she oversaw much of it, but she rarely got her hands dirty with it all. She spent far more time delegating tasks and writing reports.

"You're probably right," Beck said. "But we're still at a loss about how it happened."

"I guess we just need to wait to find out who's next. If the B-Virus is still out there, someone else will surely get it. I hate to say it, but we need more data. Two women coming down with the B-Virus is two too many, but we're going to need more spread before we can find patient zero."

"More like bimbo zero," Beck said quietly, just loud enough for him to hear himself. He did not need Alice to hear that. She probably would have laid into him, gotten angry and screamed at him for such a sexist comment, even if it was true.

Even if Alice had heard him, she could not say anything, because the phone started to ring.

"Dr. Terrapin," Alice said, answering her phone, sounding as professional as she could given the disruptive circumstances.

She listened for a moment, her jaw going slack. Then she hung up the phone without saying another word.

"What is it?" Beck asked with a knowing smirk on his face. Alice was too shocked with the news she just received to notice.

"Rose has contracted the B-Virus," Alice answered.

"Uh oh," Beck said. "We need to get you in a containment room right away. Back into the hazmat suit. I'm joining you. You were probably exposed from Rose."

Alice nodded her head, knowing it had to be true. As much as she hated donning her hazmat gear again, she saw nothing else she could do. It was for the good of everyone, both in the lab and outside, for her to go into containment. Even if she had wanted to, there was no going home for a while.

Alice found herself thankful that Beck was joining her in containment. It had already largely been proved that men were immune to the B-Virus, but with the breach in containment, it was best for them both to be careful. Alice had no idea what the B-Virus could ultimately do to a man, but if it only did half of what it did to women, the results would be catastrophic.

As soon as they both had their gear on, they stepped out of Alice's office. The route they were to take had already been cleared of people. The corridors they followed would all be thoroughly sanitized before anyone would be allowed to enter those spaces without hazmat gear of their own. Alice's office would also be completely sanitized. Even if Alice had not been exposed, there was no reason for anyone to take a chance. The containment protocols were as secure as could be.

The moment Alice stepped into the containment room, she knew something was wrong. The idea had been that each subject would spend their time alone in their own room, cut off from everyone else, completely quarantined. But When Alice and Beck entered the room, they were not the only ones there. Rose, or the woman who had once been Rose, stood in the middle of the room giggling to herself.

"We're in the wrong--"

Beck cut her off, pushing Alice deeper into the room. He shut the door behind her.

"You really aren't that smart," Beck said as he started to remove his hazmat helmet. "This whole time you've ignored the fact that you have been the common factor."

Rose turned and giggled at the sight of familiar faces. Her mind had already gone through a significant alteration, but the process was only just starting with her. Her body had not yet developed the bimbo curves that she would soon be known for.

"What are you talking about?" Alice practically screamed.

She refused to take off her helmet, just in case she had not yet been exposed like Rose had.

"First you infected Diana, your neighbor," Beck explained. "I've had men watching you since you left the lab yesterday. They kept their distance, but they saw everything, how you briefly greeted your neighbor at the mailbox. She became Didi because of you."

"And what about Jenni?" Alice cried. "I've never seen her before in my life."

"You don't remember seeing her, but that's just because you aren't particularly alert before you've had your morning coffee. You ran into her at the coffee shop. My men tracked you there as well. Luckily, no other infections have resulted from your coffee habit."

"And then Rose got it from me when we drove to pick up Didi," Alice said. "It all makes sense now. But why didn't I transform? If I'm patient zero, shouldn't I have shown signs of my infection?"

Beck shrugged his shoulders. "It turns out you're either asymptomatic or you are a carrier. There was Typhoid Mary. You might just be Bimbo Virus Alice. Although I still have hope for you."

"What do you mean?" Alice asked, now suspicious of her coworker.

"I was the one who dosed you. That's why I had men follow you. I expected you to turn into a bimbo. Only you didn't. I always thought we needed forced trials with the B-Virus. We can only do so much with cell cultures and computer simulations. Sometimes you need to see how a virus actually responds to people."

"You're a monster," Alice cried.

However, before she could further lay into Beck, her attention was drawn back to Rose, who still stood in the middle of the room giggling away as if she did not have a thought in her head. But the physical transformation had started. This was the first time the lab researchers had been able to watch a B-Virus transformation take place in person. There were cameras all over the room, currently all aimed at Rose.

It started with her chest. It was hard to see at first, her blouse and sweater doing a good job of minimizing the appearance of her chest. But with each passing moment her chest got bigger and bigger, almost as if balloons had been inserted into her breasts and someone was filling them up with an air pump. Only Rose's breasts had no balloons in them and they were not filling with air. It was the B-Virus doing its work, beginning the transformation that would forevermore leave her as a bimbo.

Once Rose's chest growth started in earnest, other parts of her body changed as well. Her butt started to expand in much the same way as her chest. Soon her pants were pulled tight across her ass, giving the appearance that they had almost been painted on. Rose's lips plumped up too, giving her the cocksucking lips that would forevermore define the type of woman she was. Their purpose was clear and no one would ever listen to what came out of her mouth again. All that mattered was what went into her mouth, with cum being the primary condiment.

As Rose's body growth finally started to slow, there was no doubt what she looked like. No one would assume she had a thought in her head. Her whole body had been remade with sex in mind. It would be almost impossible for her to continue in her job as it were, her whole body now calling out to her with new directives. Even if her mind had not been simplified, it would only take a few weeks before she gave into the demands of her body, becoming the slut that she now appeared to be.

But it was the mental changes that now became most prevalent. Alice watched in horror as whatever was left of Rose's intelligence simply sank away. Her eyes became glassy, unseeing. It was because there was nothing left going on in her mind.

Rose was not brain dead, but she was as close as could be without actually being dead. She had fully become one of the bimbo zombies, still alive, but with nothing going on in her head beyond the most basic of functions.

"Master," Rose said the moment her eyes fixated on Beck. She dropped to her knees and looked up at him reverently, as if he was a god to her. And in a way, she was.

"Good girl, Rosie," Beck said as he stepped forward and petted the newfound bimbo on the head like she was a pet.

"This is sick," Alice said. "You infected all of these women just because you wanted to get to me."

Beck shrugged his shoulders. "I'll admit, I just wanted you when I started, but I can't complain about having a little harem of my own. Four bimbos who only have eyes for me. How can I pass that up?"

"Who are the other three?" Alice asked, still seething.

"Let's fix that," Beck said. He pulled out a walkie talkie and pushed the talk button. "Open the door and bring in the other two."

Alice looked toward the main door for the room, but it did not move. The containment rooms were set up similarly to hotels with doors between individual rooms. There had been a reason for that at some point, but they were rarely used anymore. But they came in handy as the side door opened to reveal two busty beauties. Jenni and Didi sauntered into the room and made a bee-line toward Beck.

The duo dropped to their knees beside Rosie and looked up with awe in their eyes. They really did see this man as a god. He was their master.

"Good girls," Beck said, patting both of their heads in turn.

The women's clothes looked like they were about to pop. What remained of their previous normal outfits had nearly been shredded from the expansive effects of the B-Virus. And Alice was certain, no matter what she did, they would not pull their attention away from Beck. They only had eyes for him.

"This is how you wanted me to be?" Alice asked, almost spitting with fury.

Beck turned and smiled. "Don't they look happy like this? There's not a thought in their heads except the overwhelming desire to please me. This is how it should be. This is how all women should be."

"I hate you, you sick pig," Alice screamed before she ran for the door. She tried to open it, but the locks had been engaged from the outside. She was stuck. There was no escape. She was trapped with the three bimbos and their master, a man who she had once considered a colleague, even someone she might be romantically interested in. But all of that was past. He had shown her his true colors. Knowing what she knew now, she would turn him down even if he was the last man alive. Nothing could bring her to succumb to his desires.

However, as Alice struggled with the door handle, even going so far as to bang on the door and hoping someone would release her, Beck used the opportunity to make his move with her back turned. He approached silently from behind. But Alice felt Beck's approach and she tried to spin out of his grasp. Only he was not trying to grab her. He was trying to grab her helmet. He succeeded.

As Alice spun away from her captor, her helmet twisted off, coming free entirely. Her safety had been compromised. She could not assume she would be safe from infection any longer. Just because she carried the virus, it did not mean she was immune. It just meant that the level of virus in her body was not high enough to cause infection, even while she managed to spread the virus to others.

"It's probably safe to hang around Didi," Beck said, "but I wouldn't be surprised if Rosie's recent transformation meant you were exposed to enough of the virus to start your transformation. But we'll see. I've got nothing but time before we find out if you will get infected by the B-Virus like the rest of my girls here."

Alice sank back against the door and dropped to the floor. This was it. She had been exposed, actually for a second time. She could only hope her body could hold off an infection. If she could, it meant she would have plenty of time to kill Beck. If not, then she supposed she would join the other women on their knees as they worshiped Beck.

Alice remained surprisingly stoic in the face of her imminent bimbofication. She found herself in a binary situation. She either turned into one of those bimbo zombies or she remained as she was. As much as she wanted to remain Alice, she knew that if she did transform, it would not be long before she was happily worshiping Beck. At that point, it did not matter anymore.

It took nearly an hour before Alice started to feel different. She had kept her eyes closed as the other three women took turns sucking on Beck's cock. They were loud and obnoxious about it, but Alice had been able to tune them out. But by tuning out the bimbos, it meant Alice was even more observant of her own body. She paid attention to every sensation, wondering if it could be the precursor to a full blown infection.

No one had done any research on the transformation itself. No one, except the three women worshiping Beck's cock, had gone through a full transformation. The computer simulations had given a good approximation of what might happen, but considering they had never predicted a carrier like Alice, they all had to be taken with a grain of salt.

Alice could feel the heat building up in her body. It was a familiar sensation, one she experienced in the past when she got the flu or other serious illness. It was her body building up an immune response. It had found an enemy to fight. Only, this enemy could still replicate as it wished to. She had no immunity.

Beck had been involved in developing a vaccine for the B-Virus. That had been his area of expertise. But now Alice was beginning to wonder if he had actually been doing his job. Clearly he had planned to make Alice into a bimbo. And the other employees at the lab, other than Rose, seemed to be going along with it.

Suddenly Alice started giggling. It was the strangest feeling. There was nothing to prompt the giggling outburst, but it happened nonetheless. Rose had done the same before her physical transformation started. She had stood there giggling for minutes on end, completely ignoring everything else going on around her.

Alice still managed to look up and see Beck smiling at her. He knew what had happened just as well as Alice did. She had finally been infected. She had gone from carrier to infected and that meant she was going to turn into another one of those stupid bimbo zombies.

The heat inside Alice's body continued to build, except, more and more, the heat seemed to build up deep in Alice's belly, right above the junction between her legs. She wanted to reach her hands down and touch herself. Even being in a room with other people could not dampen the arousal she felt. But try as she might, she could not move her hands. She could not move her body. She was completely frozen in her place, leaving her unable to attend to her needs.

Alice kept giggling, but really, she wanted to scream. But the giggling had become involuntary. She could not stop herself. And could not speak or make another noise of any kind. There was just more giggling.

Her mind was starting to break. That much was sure. The more Alice tried to fight her confinement, the worse it got. She could feel it coming. It was a bit like approaching a cliff. As long as she kept her feet on the ground, she remained safe and able to think. But as soon as she made the leap off the cliff, there would be no more ground. There would be nothing to support her at all. She would forevermore be in free fall, stuck in her own mind, trapped and unable to actually think for herself anymore. She would be a bimbo then.

But before her mind could completely break, her body started to transform. Beck left his three bimbos to watch Alice more closely. He picked her up off the floor and stood her on her own feet. Somehow, she could not move herself, but that did not stop Beck from repositioning her however he liked. He even managed to find her balance point so that she did not fall down.

The heat that first built up inside of her started to move around her body. It congregated in her chest and around her butt most, but she could feel it all over her body. Not being able to move, Alice could not watch her body transform, but had she been able to watch herself in a mirror, she would have seen her breast blow up larger than any of the other bimbos. Her tits, for at that size, they could no longer just be considered breasts, grew to such a size that they were bigger than her head.

Alice's ass expanded almost as much to provide counter balance to an otherwise top-heavy frame. Her pants stretched beyond their breaking point, the seams splitting to reveal shredded panties over perfect skin. Her blouse also suffered, with buttons popping off and her bra simply breaking under the pressure of her expanded assets.

Of course, none of this was visible beneath the hazmat suit. Beck would have loved to see it all more closely, but even he was denied that. But he did get to enjoy watching Alice's face rebuild itself. Her lips were the most noticeable change with how they plumped up until it was no longer clear if Alice would be able to speak again. Her mouth opened slightly, creating a natural O shape between her lips. She was set to become the perfect receptacle for cock.

But it was not just her lips that changed. Alice's whole face went through a transformation. Her nose shrunk down into a perfect button nose. Her cheekbones rose and became more prominent. Then her eyes grew bigger and her eyelashes grew longer. Her eyebrows thinned and grew higher, becoming high arches that would forever leave Alice looking like she was confused.

Alice's skin became perfectly smooth, every imperfection disappearing as a deep tan formed all over her body, every inch of her skin sporting the same color. And then there was Alice's hair. With the other women, the B-Virus had left their hair alone. But Alice had received a second dose. Once her ability to act as a carrier was overcome, she had too much virus in her body and it had to do something. Her once short dark hair lightened and lengthened until she sported a long blonde mane of hair that would forevermore help define her as a dumb blonde bimbo.

Throughout all of this process, Alice had tried to mentally fight against what was happening to her, but to no avail. There was nothing she could do. She could not move. She could not speak. All she could do was ride the wave of the transformation process. Some of what happened to her she could guess at. She could feel the change in her center of gravity. She could feel how her tits pulled her forward. That improved a little when her ass expanded to match, but she still felt a gentle pull forward nonetheless. But the rest remained a mystery.

But as the physical transformation finished, Alice felt herself approaching the mental cliff. She had assumed the world beyond the cliff edge would be dark and scary, but instead it looked pink and fluffy, like she would be wrapped up in warm and comforting clouds. Even as she knew the inevitability of her future as a bimbo, Alice acted for the first time with the virus. She ran and leaped off the cliff and out into the open air. The pink clouds caught her and carried the woman that had been Alice away. In her place was just another bimbo.

To Beck's eye, he watched Alice's eyes fade. Her intelligence was gone. There was only the bimbo left. The virus had finished its work.

"Welcome, Ali," Beck said.

The newly minted Ali looked up at Beck and smiled as best she could. Her face was not designed for many expressions. It remained largely frozen. But it was nonetheless clear that Ali was happy and looking forward to serving her master.

"Hi, Master," she responded with a heavy lisp. No matter how long she lived like this, she would never be able to overcome the effect of having such prominent lips. The lisp was permanent.

"Ali, I want to welcome you to my harem by fucking you while you take turns licking the other girl's pussies."

"Yes, Master," Ali said. She started stripping off her clothing without a second thought. First the hazmat suit came off, revealing her new curves for the first time for all to see. Then she pulled off what remained of her regular clothing. Beck enjoyed every step as she disentangled herself from what had been a fully professional outfit once. Now it was but a shadow of its former self. He knew that his bimbo would never wear anything like that again. None of them would. He just needed to take a few measurements and order new outfits for her and the others.

As soon as Ali was nude, she climbed up on the bed and positioned herself on her hands and knees, presenting her ass toward her master. The other three bimbos followed orders and positioned themselves on the bed in front of Ali, their own clothes now discarded as well. They spread their legs, giving access to Ali so that she could begin her work.

However, Ali did not start right away. She looked back over her shoulder to see Beck approaching. His pleasure came first. It always came first. She would happily never cum again if it meant it kept her master happy. But the moment Beck slid his hard cock into Ali's wet and waiting pussy, she set to work.

Rosie was the first of the bimbos to receive a tongue lashing from Ali. Jenni was next. And then finally Didi. They all came quickly, their bodies always primed for sex. Ali was cumming too, over and over again as Beck railed her from behind, filling her pussy with each and every thrust. Ali might not have known that this was going to be her future, but now that she was here, she could think of nothing better. Then again, she did not have a thought in her head. Almost everything she did required an order from her master. Luckily, Beck was there to make sure she and the other bimbos always knew what they needed to do.

Afterward, once Ali's pussy had been packed full of cum, Beck sat on the edge of the bed. He had managed to put pants back on and had even managed to pull his shirt over his shoulders, but had not yet gotten around to buttoning it up yet. Ali sat on his right hand side as his senior and chief bimbo. She looked up at him with awe and sexual reverence. The other bimbos surrounded him, giving him similar looks. This was who all four women were now. They no longer had thoughts of their own. Only their master gave them thoughts.

When the door to the room was finally opened, a young man stepped inside. Beck looked at him and smiled, but the bimbos did not look away from their master. They only had eyes for him.

"The quarantine is over," the man said. "You can all come out now."

"Great," Beck said with a knowing smile. "I think I'm going to take my ladies home with me. When I return, we can get started on figuring out how to release this into the general public. This is how women should be from now on. Don't you think so?"

The young man nodded his head enthusiastically. There was

an intern working in another part of the lab that he had his eye on. He thought she would make a perfect bimbo. Little did he realize that the success of the B-Virus ultimately came down to Alice, patient zero, or as Beck preferred to think of her, bimbo zero. Alice may not have thought life as a bimbo was for her, but Ali could not imagine a better life than she now lived. And that was all that really mattered.

THE LEGEND OF THE WEREBIMBO

1

"Oh yes," Kiki moaned as my tongue darted across her clit. She took a moment of pause before she resumed licking my pussy. She had a talented tongue and I was very much enjoying her ministrations as we ate each other out. "Lydia, your tongue feels so good in my little cunny."

I almost wanted to laugh at Kiki's choice of words. There was no doubt in my mind that she was a bimbo. Usually I didn't go for the dumb blondes I came across, but there was something about Kiki that seemed endearing. And, at the very least, she was hot as fuck. With the big tits, the narrow waist, the plump ass and thick lips, I was expecting her to prefer men, but walking into a lesbian bar made her preferences known.

I had been sitting at the bar, slowly working my way through a flight of beers, when Kiki sat down beside me. She set into the seduction straightaway.

"I love your eyes," she said, although sounding a little drunk.

That was enough to get my attention, especially with how cute she sounded with her high pitched and breathy voice. There was a softness to her, beyond the incredible softness of her breasts, that I immediately found appealing.

I'll be honest. I wasn't expecting to pick anyone up at the bar. I just came in for a drink to help me unwind from another day on the force. Getting promoted to police detective was great, but it also meant I saw some gross shit sometimes. I had always been a bit squeamish when it came to blood and guts and there had been a series of bloody crime scenes to investigate as a result of a new organized crime gang muscling its way into the city. But when faced with a beauty like Kiki, it was hard to say no. Her body instantly set mine alight.

Before I knew it, she was suggesting I take her home with me for some more personal fun. I was already too turned on to deny that thought. The idea of having this woman in my bed was better than almost any of my fantasies. And with my inhibitions already lowered from my drinking, there was no way I could say no.

The funny thing, though, was we never made it to my bed. We barely made it inside my apartment before Kiki practically tackled me. It seemed she was as turned on as I was, maybe even more so. She pinned me against the door as soon as I closed it and kissed me hard on the lips. I kissed her back with a hunger I rarely felt, but had always wished to release. It seemed like Kiki's every touch of my body drove me to want more. I loved it.

We at least made it to the couch. Kiki had quickly worked to disrobe me, pulling at my pants and top until I was down to just my underwear. Not that the cotton underwear I had worn did much to stop her from leaving me completely nude. My bra and panties soon followed the rest of my clothes into a pile on the floor before she pushed me down onto the couch.

I watched with rapt attention as Kiki removed her dress. It turned out she wasn't wearing anything underneath it. Her breasts popped into view, looking round and magnificent. She looked like a porn star and as turned on as I was, I was all for it. Her pussy was bare and was already dripping wet. I had never considered myself all that attractive, but clearly Kiki had the hots for me almost as much as I had the hots for her.

Kiki climbed on top of me, straddling me and resuming the hot kisses from before. My hands roamed over her body, touching and squeezing every bit of flesh I could manage. Her tits were clearly fake, but they remained soft and pliant to my touch. Her ass was a perfect bubble butt and had the perfect mix of fat and muscle. I couldn't help but smack her ass, making her moan into my mouth as she refused to break the kiss.

But the kiss was eventually broken. And once it was, the real fun started. Kiki managed to turn around, still straddling me. She spread my legs apart and dove in with her pierced tongue. I bucked under her initial onslaught, my body unable to withstand the pleasure she provided. But after my first orgasm of the night, I soon managed to return the favor, diving into her pussy with an almost equal amount of gusto.

Kiki moaned and eventually began to encourage me with her words. I loved it. She loved it. This was a perfect night for two lesbian lovers. I had never had much luck with hookups in the past. They usually went nowhere. But I was already thinking that having someone like Kiki around more often, maybe even approaching her about having a relationship, would be something to seriously consider. That was if she was willing to get tied down to someone like me.

Deep down, I knew Kiki was a slut. With her body built as it was, with the way she dressed in a tight blue strapless dress that barely covered her incredible assets, it was assumed that she liked sex. She was definitely not my usual type, let alone a good example of the normal patronage of that specific bar. But I wasn't going to complain about fucking such a pretty and sexy woman. She was built like sex on heels and I supposed I could use some of that in my life.

We each came over and over again. Kiki was an expert, playing my body like a musical instrument, making me cum again and again. I was not nearly as skilled as a lover, but Kiki's body was so well primed for sex, I had no trouble making her cum too. I tried to give as good as I got, but even though my sexual prowess could not compare to hers, she still screamed out in orgasm as often as I did. It was fantastic.

"Oh, Kiki," I moaned as I worked through another stellar orgasm. "Where have you been all my life?"

Kiki only paused for a moment, just long enough to giggle. Then she dove right back in, forcing every thought from my mind as she drove me toward another incredible orgasm. This woman would be the death of me if I wasn't careful, but I didn't care. I loved it. She gave me everything I needed and so much more.

2

I woke up to my phone ringing. I found myself still naked on my couch, although it seemed Kiki had managed to find a blanket to cover me with. Unfortunately the little bimbo was nowhere to be seen. She was gone, disappearing into the night before I could even get her number.

"Damn," I said, regretting nothing from the night before except for the fact I had no way of contacting Kiki again. And after a late night of wonderful sex with such an incredible sexy and beautiful bimbo, I was hooked, wanting more of that in my life.

I managed to find my pile of clothes just before the call went to voicemail.

"Hello?" I said, not even nothing to look at the caller ID.

"Lydia?" came the familiar voice of my partner, Detective Jorge Gonzalez. "I know it's early, but we just got a big case. All signs point to a massive gang battle last night. We've been called in to investigate."

I sat there, trying to think, trying to get my mind to kick into gear. A gang battle probably meant a lot of blood. That was definitely not high on my list of things to deal with first thing in the morning.

"Lydia?" my partner said again. "Is everything all right?"

"Yeah," I finally said, returning to the present and the conversation on the phone. "Yeah, I'm here. Everything's fine. You woke me is all. Text me the address. I'll be there as soon as I can."

"Thanks," Jorge said. "I'll see you soon."

As soon as the call was over, I sat up and ran my hand over my face, trying to finish waking up. I needed to hurry. Jorge was depending on me. But all it took was one sniff of my body to know that I needed a shower before I showed up at the crime scene. I could smell the sex on me. Jorge was cool with who I was and who I fucked, but that wasn't true of everyone on the force. The last thing I needed was to show up smelling of sex. I would never live it down.

I showered as quickly as I could. I always kept a set of clothes ready for emergency calls. This technically wasn't an emergency, but I was in enough of a rush that I treated it as one. I didn't bother with makeup or anything like that. I knew other female detectives did, but that had always seemed like overkill unless I was called into court to testify. That was the only time I truly cared about my appearance. The rest of the time I just needed to look presentable and commanding.

I pulled up to the address Jorge texted me. The crime scene had already been cordoned off with yellow police tape. People had started to gather, either wanting to know what happened or hoping to see a dead body. Either could be true given some people's proclivities. I never understood some people's fascination with death and the recently deceased, but I wasn't a good judge of such matters.

I flashed my badge at one of the officers tasked with keeping the crowd at bay. "Detective Lydia Frost," I said. He lifted the police tape and I ducked under. I could already spot

Jorge standing at the entrance to an alley, clearly waiting for me.

"What have we got?" I asked as I approached.

Jorge held out a cup of coffee for me, which I accepted happily. There hadn't been time to brew my own or stop on the way. Jorge knew how much I loved my coffee and how much I needed it to do my best work. I drank several cups per day usually, but more when the caseload was high.

"This is a strange one," Jorge said as he led me into the alley. "No bodies, no shell casings, but a shit ton of blood. We think it was a gang fight, but honestly we don't know. I've already asked forensics to double check that we're dealing with human blood and not animal blood."

I nodded my head as I surveyed the scene for the first time. The street on the far end of the alley had also been blocked off. Additional police were stationed down there. However, whatever happened last night seemed to be confined to the alley itself.

"Any reports of gunfire?" I asked.

"You know what it's like in this neighborhood," Jorge answered. "We've got officers canvassing in the buildings, looking for witnesses, but no one's talking. They don't snitch on the organized folks here."

I nodded my head, already knowing what Jorge's answer would be. But I had to ask. Once I felt the first jolt of caffeine hit my system, I started a proper survey of the scene. There was blood everywhere, as Jorge had described. There was splatter on the walls, there were pools of it on the ground. I counted at least 15 spots where there should have been a dead body. No one could survive after the amount of blood loss experienced here. It was intense and set my stomach off. Oddly, the coffee helped settle my stomach usually, but this was almost too much.

It didn't help that all the walls of the buildings on either side of the alley were metal. With wood or brick, there would have been missed shots buried in the walls, giving us a starting point in trying to identify who did this.

Actually, before we even started, we could be pretty confident we knew who was behind this. On the one side was the already established Russian mob, led by Dmitry Rodchenkov. He was a brutal gang leader, having come to power, we believed, by murdering the previous boss. His was a reign that started in blood, which usually spelled bad things for what was to come.

On the other side was the recent activity of a new organization. Supposedly it had connections to the French mob based out of Corsica, but they were so new to the city, it was hard to have any intelligence on them. Our best guess was the gang was run by a guy named Sebastian Lambert, but we didn't even have a photo of the guy, just the name. It was tough going, but I was confident we would eventually bring both groups down. We just needed time and resources.

"Who do you think cleaned up the scene?" I asked as I bent down and looked at what looked like a ricochet mark on the concrete.

"If I had to guess, I would say it was the Lambert crew. We've never seen behavior like this from Dmitry and his crew."

I nodded my head in agreement. It was only a guess, but it was a good one.

3

Waking up, I knew something was wrong. I could sense it as soon as I returned to the waking world, even before I opened my eyes. First, there was the feel of the bed covers against my skin. They weren't my sheets. Second, I knew I wasn't wearing any clothes, as I usually wore some sort of night shirt and shorts to bed. And third, I could hear another person's breathing next to me.

I opened my eyes and turned my head to see who I had supposedly gone home with the night before. I secretly hoped it was Kiki, although I couldn't seem to remember going out and meeting her again. Actually, I couldn't remember anything from the night before. I had no memory past the time I returned home from work. But instead of Kiki's golden hair and luscious body, there was the short cropped hair and the jowls of a heavy set man.

Waking up next to this strange man left me wanting to puke in my mouth. What had happened to me? How did I get here? I didn't understand it. I never batted for the other team. I stuck to women exclusively. So why was I waking up next to his man? Had I been drugged? None of it made sense.

I sat up slowly, trying to avoid waking him. As much as I wanted answers, I didn't really want to know what happened to me. Or, more accurately, I didn't want to know what I had done. If there was any chance that what had happened to lead me to this point had been my idea or consensual, I wanted to pretend it never happened.

The man slept peacefully, as far as I could tell. His body took up most of the king-sized bed, largely because of his size. His round belly tented the covers, although I could still see his dick trying to push up and make itself known.

I shuddered at the sight. The male body had never done anything for me and I was glad that I had never even experimented with a man. But then the thought that his dick might have been inside of me at some point last night made me want to gag. I needed to get out of there.

Determined to make my escape, I moved as quickly as I dared, trying to remain as silent as the grave so as not to wake up the man who I had just shared a bed with. As soon as I had slipped out from under the covers and was standing on my own two feet, I took a moment to survey the room, trying to remember every detail. It was actually a hotel room, not a bedroom. However, that only made me more confused. Who was this man? I supposed I would need to investigate, but I wasn't sure how to completely separate my personal investigation from work. I needed to keep everything off the official books. This was private.

I looked around, trying to find clothes that I recognized, that were mine. But there weren't any. The man's clothes, as big as they were, were easy to spot. It seemed he had been wearing a suit the night before, although I had no recollection of it. His pants looked big enough to fit at least two of me in them, if not three.

Then my eyes lit upon a dress piled in the corner. There was a pair of high heels there as well. But they definitely weren't my clothes. Both items were pink. I didn't wear pink. I didn't own anything pink, clothing or otherwise. Not that I was against the color. It just wasn't for me and I avoided it whenever I could. But as I stalked around the room, on the hunt for what had to be my clothes, there simply wasn't anything else.

I wanted to curse. I wanted to scream. I wanted to rage. But there was no way I was willing to make a sound, not when the big guy was sleeping a few feet away. At least he was happily snoring. Hopefully that meant he was in a deep enough sleep so that I could make my getaway without him waking up. I crossed my fingers that was the case, at least.

I picked up the dress and held it out in front of me. I couldn't help but make a disgusted face at the dress. This really wasn't me. I was certain the dress would have looked great on Kiki, but this sort of thing was her style. It definitely wasn't mine.

However, it seemed I had no choice but to pull the dress on. I stepped into it and pulled it up my body until I was able to slide my arms through the straps. It was a simple pink cocktail dress with thin straps. It was lower cut than I would have liked and significantly shorter than anything I would ever consider wearing, but that was better than nothing. The only problem was the dress was clearly designed for someone with a bigger bust. The front looked like it just hung off of me when it should have been tight against my breasts.

I bit my lip to keep from cursing my situation. And it only got worse when I realized the shoes that had been left for me were monumentally high. I knew why women wore high heels, but I had never understood how women could physically wear heels this high without falling over. I felt like a complete klutz once I slipped my feet into them. I was sure they looked good, but they were almost impossible to walk in.

I scanned the room one last time, looking for anything that belonged to me. I didn't even see a purse or a phone that looked like mine. There was nothing.

Shaking my head, I walked out of the hotel room, being careful to not let the door slam behind me. I was free of the man, but I still needed to get home.

As I rode the elevator down to the lobby, I felt very self-conscious. If anyone I knew saw me dressed like this, especially anyone I knew from work, I honestly didn't know what I would do. I figured I would have to quit and move elsewhere, getting a job with another department, because there was no living this down, given my known reputation.

But then there was the matter of actually getting home. I had no phone. I had no money. And there was no way I was walking across town in the dress and heels. I needed a taxi.

"Excuse me," I said as I walked up to the front counter. The clerk eyed me up and down as I approached. He probably assumed I was a hooker or something like that. I didn't want to imagine what dirty thoughts were running through his mind. "Could you call me a cab? And you can tell them that I don't have money on me, but I will have it for them at my destination." I figured it was smart to be upfront about this sort of thing.

"Sure thing, ma'am," the clerk said. He might have thought I was a prostitute, but at least he was still professional about it all. And soon I would be home, putting this awful morning behind me. That was all I wanted.

4

I made it home from the hotel, although I had to put up with the taxi driver staring at me in his rearview mirror the entire drive, but that couldn't be helped. And you can be sure that I didn't provide much of a tip for that behavior. I tipped him just enough to apologize for having to make him wait while I hurried up to my apartment to grab some cash to pay him.

I took a long hot shower as soon as I was able. I needed to get the feeling of filth off my body before I could really go about my day. I scrubbed at my skin furiously, trying to get every ounce of dirt and grime I might have picked up while I was blacked out. But as I did, I tried to push all thoughts about what had happened out of my head. I didn't want to think about it. I didn't want to know what I had done or how I got there.

Rationally, I knew I should have tried to figure out what happened to me, at least so I could avoid it in the future. I probably should have gone to the hospital to get a blood sample tested, just in case I was drugged. Not that whatever drug had led me to that man's hotel room was necessarily still in my system. I was familiar with the washout periods of the various drugs that could cause my blackout. None were in my favor.

When I finally stepped out of the shower, having wrapped a towel around my head and another around my body, I heard my phone ringing. Somehow I had managed to leave it at home, along with my purse and everything else that could have identified me. It was all so confusing, especially when there were no call records that would have drawn me out of my apartment last night.

I rushed to answer the phone. It was the ringtone I had assigned to Jorge, so that meant it had to be work related.

"What's up, Jorge?" I asked. I had to hope I wasn't getting called out to another case. The gang shootout without bodies or shell casings was already going to be a bitch to solve. Just because we had a working theory of who was ultimately responsible, we had no way to prove it yet. And the proof, if it existed, would take a long time to gather.

"We're up for another case," Jorge said.

"Fuck," I cursed. "Already? We've already got the gang shootout."

"The chief wants us on this new case," Jorge answered. "He's taking away the shootout."

I hated it when the chief meddled with our cases like that, but to be honest, considering we were looking at about 15 dead bodies, even if we didn't know where they were, that case, which was really 15 cases, would have seriously hurt our case closing average if it didn't get solved, which I doubt it would have. In a way, the chief was doing us a favor.

"I suppose that's fair," I said. "What do we got on this one?"

"Dead guy in a hotel room," Jorge answered. "It's at the Crown Hotel."

"Okay," I said. "I just got out of the shower. I'll be there in 20 minutes."

However, I knew I had a bigger problem. I hadn't paid that much attention to what hotel I woke up in, but thinking back to my quick escape, it had been the Crown Hotel. At least I knew the man I had woken up beside had been alive when I left. He was snoring.

I quickly dried off and got dressed, going as fast as I could. I probably broke a few traffic laws on the way back to the hotel too, but I didn't care. Any cop that pulled me over would have let me off without an issue. We worked for the same side.

I met Jorge in the lobby. He handed me the obligatory cup of coffee, although I probably didn't really need it this morning. The adrenaline boost I had gotten from waking up in a strange man's bed had been enough to get me going. However, that boost could wear off at any time, so the caffeine was welcome.

"Someone on the cleaning staff found the body," Jorge explained as we rode the elevator up to the fifth floor. I hadn't paid attention to what floor I had woken up on, but I hoped it wasn't the fifth floor.

Stepping off the elevator, the hallway was crowded with cops. Murders always brought out big numbers, partly to protect the scene, but I had a feeling a lot of beat cops liked the thrill of being at a crime scene. And I had to figure a lot of them were hoping to catch a detective's eye, looking for a good word when promotion time came. Having once been in their shoes, I much preferred being a detective than playing the role of low-level enforcer on the streets.

As soon as we stepped into the hotel room with the body, I knew I was in trouble. One glance around the room told me all I needed to know. I saw the oversized pants draped over a chair, the pair that I figured could fit two or three of me inside. Then there was the familiar sight of the man's rotund belly. It was him. I could barely look at what had happened to him. His throat had been cut, either by a knife or with a piece of wire. To be honest, I didn't want to know.

I was squeamish about such things naturally, but this was one instance when I couldn't even begin to look at the man's face. I couldn't look at the blood which pooled around him. He had been murdered. It was obvious.

"Do we have security camera footage?" I asked one of the cops standing guard over the scene.

"The hotel was in the middle of an upgrade of their systems," the cop answered. "None of the cameras were operational last night or this morning, whenever this happened."

"Shit," I said, playing the role of cop. Inwardly, I was relieved. It meant no one would have seen me when they looked through the tapes. I didn't need any heat getting brought down on me.

"Cause of death looks to be pretty obvious," Jorge said. "Obviously the medical examiner will have his say. I wonder how long he's been dead for?"

I shrugged my shoulders. I knew it couldn't have been for that long. I was probably three hours removed from being here earlier. That didn't give the killer much time, but it didn't take much time to cut a man's throat.

"I think I'm going to be sick," I said as I rushed out of the room. I wasn't really. I just felt like I needed to get out of there. I needed space to think. Jorge let me go, knowing my aversion to blood and guts. Maybe becoming a murder detective wasn't the best career choice.

5

With me being useless to the investigation in the hotel room, I decided to go around asking some questions. My first stop was the hotel bar. It technically wasn't open yet, but there were a few employees getting it ready for a lunchtime opening. I walked in, hoping someone from last night was there this morning to answer some of my questions.

"We're not open yet," came the call of the man behind the bar.

I pulled out my badge. "I'm detective Lydia Frost. There was a murder upstairs discovered this morning. I was wondering if anyone working this morning was also working here last night?"

"Yeah, I was here," the bartender said. He spoke with a light Irish accent. "The name's Liam."

Liam set down the bottles of liquor he was stocking and motioned for me to take a seat at the bar. I sat, just so I could more easily collect my thoughts. Jorge and I had texted each other after I left the room upstairs. He sent me a picture of the man's ID. He was Roger Landy. The folks back at the station were running a background check on the guy, at least I had a reasonably good photo of him to show to the bartender.

"Was this man here last night?" I asked. I showed Liam the picture on my phone.

The bartender studied the photo for a moment. Then his eyes lit up.

"Yeah, he was here last night," Liam answered. "He was a big guy, as I recall. At first I thought he was just going to be one of those loners for the night, the kind that sits at the bar, slowly drinking himself into oblivion. I guessed he was a business traveler. I didn't see a ring on his finger, but I would guess he was probably recently divorced. Just a hunch."

I nodded as I took notes. This was a good lead. And I liked hearing that he was alone. Not that it helped me figure out how I ended up in his bed.

"But then this hot chick showed up and she was all over him," Liam continued. My heart sank, although there was no way anyone could call me a hot chick, so there was that.

"Can you describe her?" I asked.

"Look, you're a woman, so I don't want to be disparaging, but this woman looked like a total bimbo. She had big fake tits and a nice ass, all packed into a tight little pink dress. From the moment she stepped into the bar last night, she only had eyes for the man you're asking about. I don't know what it was about him that attracted her to him. Part of me wondered if she was a hooker, but he seemed as surprised by the situation as any. Although, like any man, there was no way he was going to turn down a woman who looked that hot."

Somehow Liam's description of the woman reminded me of Kiki. She had a body like he described, although when I picked her up at that bar, she had been wearing a blue dress.

"What color was her hair?" I asked, trying to get a better gauge of who this mystery woman was. I also wanted to make sure it wasn't Kiki. Not that I had a way of contacting Kiki if it was. I could only hope to find her at that bar again.

"She was a brunette, but her hair was long and silky, like you see in those shampoo commercials. I honestly didn't believe women's hair could really be like that. Like I said, she was hot. I think every man in the bar last night was wondering how the fattest man here could score such a hot piece."

Oddly, I felt the same way about Kiki. How had I been so lucky as to score her for a night of fun? But I couldn't let myself get hung up on Kiki. She likely had nothing to do with this case. However, the woman's pink dress, the one that was currently sitting in the back of my closet on the floor, where I had put it upon returning home, sounded a lot like the dress this woman had worn last night. That was a bit scary, but there was no way I was this mystery woman. The lake tits alone precluded that. We were both brunette, but that was the only similarity between us from what I could tell.

"I assume the two eventually left together?" I asked. It was the natural conclusion of their encounter.

"Oh yeah," Liam said. "I have no doubts he got lucky last night. I mean, if I had to die, it sure would be nice to go out fucking a hot piece of ass like that."

Liam had given up on trying to remain fully professional, but I could sense that he was a bit enamored with the woman. He probably went home and jacked off to his memory of the woman, putting himself in Mr. Landy's place. I figured most men would.

"Do you have an idea when the pair might have left the bar last night?" I asked. Timing was everything in murder cases.

Liam shrugged. "Not exactly. It wasn't late or anything. The guy probably sat down at the bar around eight. The woman showed up maybe around nine. They were probably here together for about an hour, maybe a little longer, before they left. But that's just a guess. I just know that we had last call at one and everyone was out by two."

Those were standard bar operating hours in the city. Even though I doubted the bartender had been so strict about the timing, he was smart enough to not admit to it. And rankly, considering I wasn't interested in his operating hours, I didn't care if he fudged the liquor license rules.

"You've been a great help, but I've got one last question," I said. "I understand the hotel security system was getting upgraded last night and there isn't any footage from the hotel. Is the bar on the same system or do you have your own?"

Liam shook his head. "Same owners. Same system. Sorry, I can't help you more than answering questions."

"No, you've been a great help," I said. "Thanks. If you think of anything else, here's my business card."

I handed Liam my card and then walked back toward the elevator. Jorge was still upstairs and I needed to fill him in with what I learned. However, I was thankful that nothing so far had pointed to me. I still had no answers for myself, but I at least knew I wasn't going to turn into a suspect anytime soon.

6

I woke up groggy and confused. I opened my eyes and that condition got no better. I wasn't in my bed. I wasn't in my apartment. I wasn't even in a bed for that matter. I was on some crusty old couch.

"Fuck," I said as I rubbed my head. There was a pounding behind my eyes, like a hangover, but I was pretty sure I hadn't been drinking. Then again, I had no idea where I was.

I sat up and assessed my situation, ignoring the fact I didn't know where I was. I needed to make sure I was okay first. But the moment I looked down I wished I hadn't. I wore a dress, but it wasn't a dress I had ever seen before. Like the pink dress I had woken up with when I woke up beside Roger Landy. I still hadn't figured that whole situation out yet. And this just added another layer to that mystery.

My dress was black this time, but it was horribly skimpy. I never would have worn it in a million years. But it was short and it also sported a huge cutout that started just above my breasts and went all the way down to my navel. To make matters worse, the dress was so short that it barely covered my ass. And in case there was any wondering, I wasn't wearing panties. I could feel the cool air against my slit.

This was bad. I knew that from the start. I had somehow blacked out again. But it was also clear to me that I was wearing clothes that belonged to a bustier woman. The dress was tight, but not tight enough around my chest and it even felt a little loose around my butt.

But the worst of all was the shoes. They were tall platform heels, the kind stripper wore. I had never worn anything like them before and I had never even been tempted. I thought the pink heels I had worn home from the hotel had been high. These added six or maybe even eight inches to my height. It was insane. How did women walk in these?

At least I knew I wasn't hurt. I had no memory of the night before, but I was alone and presumably safe for the moment. The couch I woke up on was covered in brown leather. But when I looked around the room, trying to figure out where I was, I realized I didn't want to know what people got up to on the couch.

I was clearly in the backroom of some business. There was a card table in the middle of the room with six chairs surrounding it. There were beer bottles and tumbler glasses on the table. I had not spent the night completely alone, it seemed. People had been here playing cards and drinking. Or at least that was my assumption. Had I been playing cards? That was hard to believe given the outfit I was wearing. But I didn't want to think about what else I might have done.

As I sat there, I slowly started to realize some of the pounding in my head was not from a hangover—although part of it still was—but actually from the pounding of bass music nearby. It took me a moment, but then I suddenly put it all together. I was in the back room of some sort of club. Not that I wanted to know what kind of club. When it came to my own sanity, there were some things I didn't want to know.

I pushed myself to my feet and slowly found my balance. Again, I wondered how women walked in these shoes. I considered taking them off, but I didn't really want to walk around barefoot. I didn't know what had been spilled on this floor before. I took a tentative step and nearly fell on my ass. But I kept at it and eventually I managed to maintain an unsteady gait.

Now it was time to leave. There was a single door. I walked over toward it, feeling as awkward as could be, especially the way my heels kept clicking and clacking on the floor. It was a good thing I was alone. If this had been like at the hotel room, even with a carpeted floor, I was afraid I would have woken the man.

The door was unlocked. I opened it slowly, peering outside. The door opened into a hallway. I could hear the music louder to my left. It kept pumping away, although I could hear more than just the bass line now. It still sounded pretty trashy. Across the hall stood an open door. I looked inside and saw a mirror and vanity. The room was empty, but I could see a lot of colorful outfits hung up on a rack. All of them were skimpy.

"Strip club," I said quietly to myself. I had woken up in the back room of a strip club. The only way this could get any worse was if I got caught.

To my right, at the end of the hallway, was another door. This one was closed, but it had an exit sign above it. I sighed with relief. That was my way out.

I hurried into the hallway and down toward the exit. The heels forced my ass to wiggle as I walked. It was annoying as hell, but I didn't care as long as I got out of there.

The door opened easily and I was inundated by bright sunshine. I had no idea what time it was, but it looked and felt like morning. I didn't know strip clubs opened this early, but there was probably always some stupid sucker who needed to watch skanky women dance around a pole. They probably imagined the pole was their dick. Not that I expected any man who frequented a strip club to have a big dick. But hey, everyone gets to dream.

I exited the building and found myself standing in an alley. I looked back at the door. It said Razzle Dazzle on it. I assumed that was the name of the club. I didn't want to walk around to the front to verify, just in case I ran into someone who recognized me.

Knowing I needed to get home, I walked through the alley until I reached the next street. It was busy enough that I spotted a cab. I flagged it down and got in. I didn't even care that the driver kept his eyes on me the whole time I was in his backseat. I had another long hot shower in my future. Of that I was certain.

7

Without a new case to take up my time and without the need to follow up leads in person, I decided to spend my work hours investigating the Razzle Dazzle. I wasn't familiar with strip clubs in the city, especially their ownership. The vice squad was probably more familiar, but I wasn't willing to tip my hand about what had happened. At least not yet.

I didn't understand what had happened to me. How had I blacked out? How had I ended up wearing such skimpy and slutty clothes? I had no idea what I had done while blacked out, but considering I had woken up next to Roger Landy before he died, I could only presume sex had somehow been involved. But I didn't have any actual answers. I just had conjecture.

The city planning department was across the street from police headquarters. There were other departments there as well, so I was easily able to tell Jorge that I was going to check some things out from the city records. "I have a hunch, but I need more information before I share it," I told him.

Jorge was a good guy. He was a trusting guy. I hated to lie to my partner, but there was no way I was willing to tell him what I was really investigating. Besides, if I learned something that might help our case, I would certainly find a way to share it. I just had to make sure I was protected first. I had to make sure there was no way for the information I found could lead back to me in any way.

The city planning department records were almost all part of the public record. Usually it cost money to get employees to search for you, but it had been a long-standing policy to allow the police to look through the records as long as they used their own manpower. I just flashed my badge and they waved me by. I didn't even need to sign in. And I was definitely glad of that, because I wasn't being truthful in my actions. If someone came to check on me, they would easily see through my ruse.

Not that I spent a lot of time in the planning office or the records room. I had been here twice before, both in high profile cases where other officers did the actual grunt work. I had just shown up at the right time to take advantage of their work. This time I was the one doing all the searching.

It took a few minutes to figure out the filing system. Every city is different in how they keep their records. Unfortunately, the city hadn't moved its records online or even digitized them yet. I had to do everything by hand.

"There we go," I said after finally finding the right drawer. The records room was filled with filing cabinets. That was half the battle right there. Once I figured out how the records about the strip club had been filed, I had to actually locate them. It took nearly half an hour to figure all of that out.

I opened the drawer and immediately started thumbing through the files, looking for anything that related to Razzle Dazzle. If I found what I was looking for, I would come up with some leads. That was important. I didn't expect the bad guys to use their names on the paperwork. But I knew strip clubs were great places to launder cash. They made for good ways to make dirty money appear clean again, as so much of the strip club operated as a cash business already.

It took me a moment to find the right file. The drawer was stuff to the brim with files. And it wasn't like I knew exactly what I was looking for, like how the file was labeled. But once I did, I excitedly pulled it out and began to leaf through it.

As expected, there wasn't much there. But the property had been sold within the last year. The new owner was some LLC, probably a shell company set up to separate the real owners from legal risk. If the club got sued or if it was found out, the shell company would fold, its assets protected, and another one would pop up in its place. If we were really unlucky, the owner would be able to reopen the club within a few days, citing new management, even if nothing actually changed other than the ownership company.

However, as I looked at each and every person who signed their name to the documents, I noticed they all had one thing in common. They were all French names. Even the notary had a French last name.

Not working in an organized crime specific unit, there was only so much I knew about the mob. I did know that they tended to operate like family businesses in a way, usually requiring those who took part to be of a certain ethnicity or background. To get into the higher echelons of the Italian mob, you had to have family roots in Italy. It was similar with the Russian and Irish mobs too. I could only assume it was similar with the French contingent too.

In the big picture, it didn't mean much, but it was a start. And it confirmed to me that the recent spate of murders in the city probably were connected to the French mob moving into town, fighting for territory. Knowing that the French mob at least had a connection to Razzle Dazzle was enough for me to want to keep an eye on it.

When I returned to my desk in the detective's bullpen, Jorge was already gone. He had a family at home to deal with and there were times when he had to cut out early to deal with the kids. His wife usually worked normal hours, but that just meant that Jorge was often responsible for emergencies. A kid had to stay home sick, Jorge usually did too. He had that kind of flexibility, especially when his job often forced him to work strange hours. He was given that leeway.

I was just glad that I didn't need to explain anything to my partner. I didn't like lying to him. And no matter what happened, if Jorge asked me about my search through the public records, I would have had to lie to him. I had found something. It just had no bearing on our case. Or so I figured. I didn't see a connection between our case and the strip club, even though I was connected to both through my blackouts. But I didn't want to think about that.

8

When I woke up the next morning, I was thankful to find myself in my own bed. And I remembered all of the night before too. I didn't black out. I probably would have gone crazy if it had happened again. I wouldn't have been able to handle it. I would have either turned myself in to the chief or I would have gone straight to the state psychiatric hospital and asked to be committed. That was how far I had fallen.

However, just because everything seemed normal, that did not mean I was looking forward to another day at the office trying to pour over records and look at the evidence in a new way. Admittedly, the investigation needed time for the forensic team to process all the evidence that was collected. Once that happened things would surely pick up. But the forensic lab had a backlog from the big gang fight crime scene. I was probably just spinning my wheels until then. I didn't even need the medical examiner's report. It was obvious what the cause of death was.

I called Jorge to let him know I wasn't coming into the office. I decided to use a sick day. I rarely took sick days, but I was generally pretty lucky when it came to illnesses. My immune system was strong enough to fight off most infections before they could take root.

"You must have whatever my daughter has," Jorge offered. "You probably got it from me. But it's not like a sick day will hurt anything. We're still waiting on the toxicology report and the rest of the forensics. Take the day and hopefully I'll see you tomorrow."

"Sounds like a plan," I said, adding a sniffle at the end, just to sell the bit. Not that Jorge had any idea I was lying through my teeth to him.

I really hated lying to Jorge at all. He was a good detective and he cared about people. I couldn't say the same of some of the other officers and detectives on the force, but I didn't have control over Human Resources. All I could do was keep a wary eye out for trouble and share anything inappropriate I was with the internal review team. I had been known to pass along a few tidbits before. I might have been a cop, but I held my coworkers to a high standard. I just wished I could live up to that standard at the moment.

When I dressed that morning, I chose a casual outfit: jeans and a sweatshirt. I wasn't trying to give off a specific look, but I didn't want to stand out when I showed up at Razzle Dazzle. Since waking up there, I had become obsessed with it. I knew it wasn't healthy, but I needed to know more. And I figured me walking in as a private citizen would at least allow me to blend in a bit and avoid catching anyone's eyes.

Of course, being a woman, I didn't naturally fit in with the usual strip club clientele. I wasn't a sleazy man. As a woman, I would naturally stand out, but as a lesbian, I could at least pretend that played a role in my visit. It wouldn't be a lie to tell anyone who questioned me that I liked women. And I knew a few other women who liked going to strip clubs. They just probably didn't visit as part of the lunchtime crowd.

I drove to the club, parking in the parking lot, as if I was a regular visitor. I walked in, nodding to the bouncer who didn't provide me with any hassle. Then again, I definitely looked old enough to be there and I wasn't threatening in any way. I didn't even bring my police badge with me. If I had to describe my reason for coming, it was to take part in undercover research. I was just gathering information. I wasn't doing anything that could be considered illegal.

I sat down at a table near the front stage, but far enough away that no one would be looking to me to pay out any tips. Besides, I wasn't exactly there for the dancing. I wasn't there to be entertained. I was there to watch and try to learn something about the club. And if I got to see Sebastian Lambert as part of my work, then all the better. Being able to tie him to Razzle Dazzle would be good for eventually bringing him down.

However, before I could get too comfy, the waitress came over.

"Normally I'd be asking you if you want a drink," the woman said. She looked a bit trashy, wearing a gold-sequined skirt that was far too short and a gaudy top that showed too much skin. Yes, this was a strip club, but the waitresses didn't need to be fighting for the male gaze with the strippers. However, I tried not to judge too much. I certainly wouldn't say anything to her face. Not yet at least.

"What are you going to do instead?" I asked. The woman had been thrown off her game enough she forgot to finish the conversation. This was definitely out of the ordinary. That or she just wasn't that bright to begin with. I figured it was a mix of both.

"Oh," she said, returning to her senses. "The boss wants to see you in his office. It's through the door over there. First door on your right."

"Thanks," I said as I pushed myself to my feet. The truth was, the woman on stage wasn't doing it for me anyway.

I walked through the door that clearly led toward the back

of the club. I found myself standing in a familiar hallway. It was the same one I had been in when I woke up in the poker room or whatever that had been. The pounding of the bass was a little less prominent here, which I was thankful for. The club's music selection was probably par for the course when it came to strip clubs, but I still didn't like it.

However, my heart pounded in my chest, keeping time with the music. I recognized many of the doorways ahead of me. At the very end was the exit I had used before. I could have used it again, escaping from whatever the "boss" wanted from me. However, I needed information. I needed to find out what was happening to me.

The first door on the right was closed. I walked up to it and knocked.

"Come in," came a strong masculine voice that sported a surprisingly sexy French accent.

I opened the door to find an office. The man who the sexy voice belonged to sat behind the desk. He looked at me with a knowing smirk.

"Come in Detective Frost," the man said. "Or do you prefer me to call you Lydia? Either way, let me say welcome to Razzle Dazzle. My name is Sebastian Lambert."

I didn't know what to say. When I showed up at the club, I had hoped to spot some possibly illegal activity. I never expected to get called into the back office to meet none other than Sebastian Lambert, the leader of the local French mob. This was going to be bad no matter how it played out.

9

"I can see you weren't expecting to see me," Lambert said. He motioned toward the two chairs in front of his desk. "Please, take a seat. Let's talk."

"Thank you, Mr. Lambert," I said, not knowing what else I was supposed to say to him. I briefly wondered if this was how the mob made connections with the police, turning good cops into dirty cops. I always figured that many times it was a blackmail relationship, but I could see these things beginning in other ways. Did he intend to try and turn me, to pump me for information? I had no idea. I hoped not.

"Call me Sebastian, please," he said as I took a seat. I felt awkward sitting across from him. Although as much as I would have loved nothing more than to jump across his desk, drag him down and put handcuffs on him, I wasn't here representing the police department. I didn't have handcuffs on me. I didn't even have my badge or my gun. And I had little doubt that he was armed.

"So you know who I am," I said. "I suppose that means you have been keeping tabs on the police in the city."

"Not as much as you might think," Sebastian answered.

"You see, I have other means to get the information I need. You may not realize this, but this isn't the first time we've met."

"I'm sure I would remember if we met before," I countered. And that was true. I didn't remember meeting him. I didn't remember his incredible voice or his strong jaw. If I didn't swing for the other team, he would have definitely been my type.

"Yes, I understand the amnesia that comes along with your condition to be frustrating. Although I assure you, it is only one way."

"You've lost me," I said. "I haven't experienced any amnesia before."

Yes, it was a lie, but I didn't want this man to have anything he could potentially hold over me. I never wanted to give him anything he could use against me.

"Oh, so that was you acting like a little slut at the card game two nights ago?" Sebastian asked with that annoying smirk of his. "You remember how you serviced all of my guests with your body, using your mouth, your pussy, your ass, even your tits? You were very popular."

My jaw dropped open in surprise. I mean, it should have been a surprise that it had happened, considering what I woke up to. But had I really done something like that when I was otherwise an ardent lesbian. There wasn't a man on earth, even the ones I found to be sexy, that I would willingly have sex with, in any way, shape, or form.

"And then there was the night you spent with Roger Landy," Sebastian continued. "I didn't get to see you in action that night, but I was sure you helped the fat fuck go out in style. If a man's got to go, I always feel it's best to give him something good beforehand. And I am certain a night spent with you blew his mind before it was extinguished."

"You killed him?" I stood up, half asking, half accusing.

"Me?" Sebastian said calmly. "No. You know how it works. I don't kill people. That's beneath me."

Of course it was. Sebastian wouldn't get his hands dirty when it came to such matters. There was nothing except our conversation that would lead back to him. Someone else would take the fall if it was necessary. That was how it worked. And I was certain if I tried to use this conversation against him, he would find a way to use my blackout activities against me, either to discredit me or to simply blackmail me into silence.

"But I think it's time to clue you in on what's happening to you," Sebastian continued. "But I think to help make that point, I'm going to bring in a friend of yours."

Sebastian pushed a button on the phone and started to say, "Send in Kiki, please."

It was only a moment later that the door opened and the familiar face and form of Kiki bounced into the room. She was all smiles, wearing high heels, a dark blue circle skirt that did nothing to hide the fact she wasn't wearing panties and a yellow tube top that failed to cover her navel and barely kept her tits in check, the top only reaching maybe an inch above her nipples, which tented the fabric and made it obvious how turned on she was. Her glistening slit told the same story.

Kiki waved to me, but she bounced around the desk and sat down in Sebastian's lap. His hands automatically reached up and started stroking her body, paying special attention to her tits.

"Obviously you two know each other already," Sebastian said. I simply stared at the scene unfolding in front of me with disbelief. I couldn't believe that Kiki had been working for the French mob all this time. I never would have guessed it. "It's because of Kiki that you're in this mess to begin with."

"I don't understand," I finally said. And I didn't. I was disappointed that Kiki was actually working for Sebastian. That probably meant I was targeted, but I didn't see how me taking

Kiki home would help Sebastian. I didn't keep any files at home. And the personal information I did have was all locked up. I knew Kiki wasn't smart enough to break into a safe. She was a bimbo, completely. It was obvious even now as she ground her ass into Sebastian's lap. I was a little jealous of him.

"When I brought this organization to America, I brought with it one of my family's most prized secrets," Sebastian explained. "In France it was a legend. Only my family believed it was true. Kiki is an example of that secret. She is a werebimbo. Like a werewolf, a werebimbo is a person who transforms into a bimbo. It used to be only at the full moon, but my family has managed to make a few changes with them. We have control of when a werebimbo shifts. Although, to be honest, Kiki here hasn't returned to her natural form in years."

"Nuh uh," Kiki said, shaking her head. "I love being a bimbo."

"I know you do," Sebastian said before he turned his attention back to me. "Since Kiki is a werebimbo, she has the ability to transform other women into werebimbos too. And that was what she did with you. Those nights where you blacked out, you had turned into a bimbo. Once you transformed, you needed no persuading to go give Landy the last fuck of his life. And you were excited to come here and entertain my guests the other night. You did it all willingly."

"We haven't…" I said, wanting to be sure that I hadn't actually done anything with Sebastian yet. Somehow, despite the craziness of what Sebastian told me, I didn't find it hard to believe. It answered so many of my questions and lingering doubts. It explained why the dresses I woke up with were too big for me in the chest. It explained where my missing time went.

"Not yet," Sebastian said. "However, I brought you back here to make you an offer. If you choose to go bimbo full time, like Kiki here has, I'll be sure to hire you. You make a great bimbo."

I didn't need time to decide. I knew the answer right away.

"Fuck you," I said, spitting anger in his direction. I felt violated by what he had done. He had set me up. He had used Kiki to turn me into a pawn. I wasn't going to let that happen. It was time to come clean to the chief and hope he could protect me. At the very least, I could turn evidence against Sebastian and maybe get him locked up. He had admitted to calling on the hit against Landy.

I stormed out of the office without looking back once. I needed to get to the station. It was time to confess to my sins.

10

I knew I had called in sick, but I decided to go have a sit down with the chief. I needed to fill him in on what I'd learned. Yes, I knew I was compromised, but I figured I could still be used as an asset in some way. At the very least, I could ultimately testify against Lambert, assuming a case was brought against him in a reasonable period of time.

And I couldn't forget what had been done to me. That hookup with Kiki had ultimately been my downfall. I didn't understand the whole werebimbo legend, but after what I had experienced, I didn't doubt its veracity. If I was a werebimbo, that explained my blackouts and how I ended up in places I didn't belong. I didn't know how Lambert was activating me or if he was just taking advantage of me transforming already. I didn't trust him anymore than I did before. I didn't even trust that his story was completely accurate. But there was no doubt that I was a werebimbo now.

After walking out of the strip club, I went home. I felt the need to take another shower. Strip clubs made me feel dirty, even if I wasn't there for all that long. And since I decided to go into work, I figured a change of clothes would be good as well. The last thing I needed was to show up at the station in casual clothes that probably reeked of cigarette smoke and creepy men's dreams.

By the time I finally rolled into work, it was well into the afternoon.

"Lydia?" Jorge asked as I dropped my coat off at my desk. "I thought you were out sick."

"Oh," I said, realizing I had just been called out for my earlier lie. "I'm feeling better now. I thought I should talk to the chief. But why are you here? I thought you were home with a sick kid."

"Yeah, um, about that," Jorge said. He rubbed the back of his head with his hand as he tried to figure out what to say next. "I got called in for questioning. Some of the results came back from the hotel murder. They found your fingerprints all over the place, almost as much as the victim."

"Shit," I quietly swore to myself. I hadn't thought about that. I should have come clean as soon as I found out the guy had been murdered. I had been too caught up in my blackouts and what that might mean to remember about fingerprints. I was screwed. There was no way around that.

"Look," Jorge said. "You shouldn't be here. Let department procedure run its course. I'm sure there's a good reason for your prints being there. You'll have a lawyer with you when you give your statement and get interviewed. After that, you just have to hope for the best. You're on leave until then. But if you did anything wrong, know that you're putting my career in jeopardy as much as you are yours. And I have a wife and kids to think about."

"I'm sorry," I said before I made a run for it. I had to get out of there. I grabbed my coat and ran for the door.

I was back in my car a minute later, my hands gripping the

steering wheel, my knuckles turning white, as I tried to figure out what I should do. This wasn't how I expected things to go. And the unfortunate truth was I didn't think I had a leg to stand on. I was screwed. There was no defense. I should have brought up my relationship with Mr. Landy from the start. I didn't need to say anything more than that I had met him.

Then again, I wouldn't have been any help in providing any information about him. Waking up, I didn't know who he was. And I certainly wasn't going to let the other guys on the force think that I had started switch hitting. That wouldn't end well. No, there was nothing I could have done. If I had beat the fingerprint analysis with my side of the story, I could have controlled the narrative, but it was too late for that now. Now it was obvious I had spent several hours in that hotel room with Mr. Landy. There was nothing more to say.

I eventually pulled out into traffic. My initial thought was to head home again. But the truth was, I didn't want to go home. I was a cop. I was a detective. My job was to investigate. I still didn't know enough about what had happened to me. But I also had no leads. I knew I could try returning to see Sebastian at the strip club, assuming he was still there, but he had already given me an ultimatum. Either I worked for him full time or I would continue to be compromised. I had no choice, which was just how he wanted it.

There had been a couple times when Jorge and I were just completely stuck on our cases. The backlog was starting to build up and we felt the crush of all the work we had ahead of us. I never took part in it, but Jorge had a couple times, just hoping to give us something to go on, something that would lead us to additional evidence. Jorge visited a psychic. I didn't believe in such stuff, but every time Jorge visited her, he came back with a lead. And given my situation, I figured it wouldn't hurt to see if this psychic of his could help me.

I pulled a quick U-turn, not particularly caring about the

legality of it at the moment. I needed to be driving in the opposite direction. It probably wasn't the safest maneuver, considering it was nearing rush hour, but I didn't care. I needed answers. And soon I was traveling in the right direction to receive those answers.

11

"I was expecting you, Detective," Madam Shabriri said as soon as I walked through the front door of her little shop. She stood up from a small round table, a crystal ball sitting in the middle. Despite the fact she had set up shop in a strip mall, the inside of her shop would probably give the fire marshal an aneurysm with all the curtains and other fabric hanging from the walls and ceiling. It was a fire hazard waiting to happen.

Luckily, I didn't care about any of that. I was on administrative leave. My police powers had been removed. I could make a call as a concerned citizen, but I was almost certain such a complaint would just get ignored. They usually were. It was a sad state of affairs that I had seen from the other side. I knew how things really worked and as much as I tried to make the world a better place, investigating crimes and bringing criminals and murders to justice, there was only so much I could do.

"Really?" I asked, more annoyed than anything. I didn't need this woman using her hocus pocus on me. I just wanted to know what she saw. The theatrics were unnecessary.

"The inner eye does not lie," she said, waving her arms around beneath her many layers of cloaks.

"Fine, but can we ignore the theatrics for this one?" I asked with a sigh. "I'm having a bad day. I don't need the grift. I just want to know if you can help me."

"Sure," the woman shrugged. "Have a seat and let's see what I can do for you."

It was a relief not to have her acting like she was some mystical medium. She was a person, first and foremost. But she had a talent to help people and that was what I needed. I needed help. I didn't need any of the mumbo jumbo that came with her profession.

I sat down across from Madam Shabriri, not knowing what to expect.

"Hold out your hands," she said. "I need physical contact to do my work."

I held out both hands, placing my elbows on the edge of the table.

"Thank you," she said as she reached out similarly, placing her hands in mine, letting her fingertips rest lightly in my palms.

"I—"

"Quiet," she cut me off. "Let me work."

I didn't say anything, although I thought her behavior was strange. I wasn't going to interrupt her. I wanted answers with as little effort as possible.

"I see that your life is currently in turmoil," Madam Shabriri began. "You are stuck at a fork in the road of life. Ah, I see it now. You are being pulled in two different directions by two masters. On the one side is the detective. This was your path for many years, but a new branch has formed only recently. You are hesitant to follow this new path, because it is so different from your previous one."

I had to hand it to her. She had largely pegged my situation correctly. She had described the events of the past few days, although with a certain ambiguous flair, almost perfectly.

"There is trouble at work," Madam Shabriri continued. "It is trouble that could lead to a possible and permanent end. But this new path. It provides a very different possible future. There is happiness in this future. There is wealth. There is success, although in a form that currently feels unnatural to you. Wait, I'm getting a name. The name is Mandi, spelled with an i. Mandi is happy, but she wants permanence. She wants to come out of the shadows and live her life full time."

I honestly didn't understand what Madam Shabriri was talking about. As soon as she started talking about Mandi, I got lost. Unless… Then it hit me. Mandi wasn't some random woman. She was me. She was the bimbo that came out when I blacked out. There was no way this woman could have known about the name Mandi. I didn't even know about it until she had said it, but I had no doubts that the bimbo emerged during my blackouts was named Mandi.

But there was only so much of the mysticism that I could take and I had reached my limits. I pulled my hands back, breaking the connection Madam Shabriri had made with me. I reached into my coat and pulled out a small wad of bills. I didn't know how much I needed to pay, but I just tossed the bills on the table and got up to leave. I couldn't stay here for another moment. I had to get out of there.

I quickly fled the shop and was soon back behind the wheel of my car again. Only I was once again faced with the decision of where I should go. I probably should have stayed with the psychic longer, but I couldn't stand it anymore. It probably had something to do with the name. Mandi. That was my alter ego. That was the name of the bimbo who took over when I blacked out. She was the one who slept with Roger Landy before he died. She was the one who entertained a group of Sebastian's guests during a card game.

I wanted to puke. But more importantly, I wanted revenge. The news of my being placed on leave had been given to me in a haphazard way. They should have taken my badge and my gun. Instead, I still had both. And I intended to use both to my advantage. I was going to kill Sebastian if he didn't give me my life back. It was that simple.

I put the car into gear and pulled out of the parking space. I looked up to see the reflection of my eyes in the rearview mirror. They were cold and hard, just like I felt toward the man who had tried to ruin me. But I was going to ruin him. The time for investigation was over. It was time to act. I didn't care what happened to me after this. I just needed to be rid of the evil that Sebastian had darkened my soul with. I needed to be rid of Sebastian and Kiki, and more than anyone, I needed to be rid of Mandi.

12

I stormed into Razzle Dazzle, my gun already drawn. The bouncer took one look at me and backed away. He wasn't about to mess with me.

I didn't give the stage a single glance. My eyes were rooted on the door to the back, the same door I had gone through just that morning when Sebastian called me back to meet with him. But I was done with meetings. Now it was time for some proper negotiation. And what better way to negotiate than to do it with a gun.

However, as soon as I neared the door that led into the back, my vision started to go fuzzy. My knees went weak and I slowly dropped to the floor. Everything faded to black.

When I next opened my eyes, I found myself in the dressing room I had spotted across the hall from the card room. Or at least I assumed it was that dressing room. I hadn't gotten a great look at it, but it looked like I remembered it.

"What the hell?" I said as I held a hand to my head. There was a pounding right behind my eyes. This was definitely a hangover.

Suddenly I heard giggling. I looked up, realizing I hadn't yet looked everywhere yet. Sitting in the corner, staring at me with wide eyes, was Kiki. My eyes went from looking at her blonde hair then down to her tits which were barely restrained in a bandeau top that left both the tops and bottoms of her tits on display. She clearly had no shame when it came to her body.

"What happened?" I asked, this time directing the question directly at her.

"You were so sexy out there tonight," Kiki answered. "Do you want to see?"

The events before I arrived at the club came flooding back into my mind. Anger resurfaced, fighting against the pain in my head. I had come here to kill, or at least to threaten to kill, Sebastian. I wanted my life back. But he controlled my blackouts. He saw me coming and he triggered a bimbo period. No matter what I planned or attempted to do, he could always make Mandi surface and there was nothing I could do about it. I was screwed.

"No," I said, crossing my hands over my chest. That was when I looked down to discover I was only wearing a set of little pink pasties over my nipples and the tiniest thong I had ever seen. That was it, although a pair of insanely high stripper heels were on the floor by my feet.

I looked around and spotted a thin pink robe with faux pink fur along the edges. I didn't care to wear it, but I needed something to cover me. I couldn't sit here like this. I needed some manner of modesty. I covered myself up, using the robe like a blanket, feeling slightly better about my situation.

However, while I was busy covering myself, Kiki pulled out a phone and started playing a video. She held it out to me so I could watch it.

"You make such a sexy bimbo, Mandi," Kiki said as she continued holding the phone out to me.

I couldn't help but watch. I couldn't help but see a busty brunette on stage, swinging around the pole as if she had spent all her adult life training for that one purpose. I couldn't help but watch how graceful she appeared. She was also sexy beyond reason. Her tits, her ass, her lips. She was like a brunette version of Kiki, only prettier.

When the dance ended, the video kept playing. "Another great performance by Mandi," the DJ announced before he started to introduce the next dancer.

My jaw dropped upon hearing that name. I had assumed the woman was just another one of the club's dancers. But no, that woman was me. She was Mandi, my bimbo alter-ego. After forcing me to blackout, I had spent that time as Mandi stripping. I was so embarrassed. How did this happen to me? I knew the answer, but I still felt sick at the thought that Sebastian had somehow corrupted me. I hated him all the more.

"There's another one," Kiki said as she started a second video. "This one's my favorite."

Mandi wasn't on stage this time. Instead, she seemed to be sitting on a man's lap in the audience. It looked like a bachelor party. The man's lap she sat on wore a crown that said Groom on it. Mandi was dressed like I was now, wearing a thong and the pink pasties to cover her nipples. Except, she wasn't really clothed. One hand remained near her ass. She was pulling the thong aside, leaving her open to the groom's cock. She bounced on it, fucking herself where everyone could see her.

The look on Mandi's face as she rode the cock was like pure bliss. She looked beyond happy. The groom's hands roamed over her body. If anything, she encouraged it. And then his buddies would reach out and grab a handful of flesh too, enjoying the bimbo they had at their disposal until she got called back up for another dance.

I squeezed my thighs together and could feel something shift inside of me. I could still feel the man's cum in my pussy. I made a disgusted face, sticking my tongue out, but it didn't help. All I knew was I felt dirtier than ever. An all day shower wouldn't be enough to wipe the shame I felt from my body.

"Where are my clothes?" I finally asked, knowing I needed to get dressed and make my escape. I couldn't come here anymore. That much was obvious. Sebastian could trigger a bimbo episode at any time.

"Just grab something off the rack," Kiki said pointing toward the rack of skimpy outfits hanging from the rack along the far wall. "Besides, those clothes you came in here wearing were so boring, Mandi. You should only wear sexy clothes from now on."

"Get out," I screamed.

Kiki jumped and scrambled toward the door. She hadn't expected my outburst.

"And don't call me Mandi. My name's Lydia."

Just as Kiki reached the door, she turned and looked back at me, almost afraid of what I might do to her. At least I could still scare a bimbo like her, even if I couldn't touch Sebastian.

"Fine," she said, pouting. "But Sebastian wants to see you now that you're boring again."

I gritted my teeth as I watched her leave. Of course Sebastian wanted to see me. And as long as I was stuck in the strip club, I was going to comply. But as soon as I was out, I was gone. I would flee across the country if I had to. I would do whatever it took to get and stay away from the monster that was Sebastian Lambert.

13

I didn't bother to knock before I walked into Sebastian's office. I had managed to find my old clothes, although my bra was completely shot. It seemed Mandi's growth spurt had torn it apart when I shifted last time. My pants felt a little loose around the butt too, but I figured that was from getting stretched out. Luckily, there was no other damage. Although I couldn't find my panties and ended up continuing to wear the pink thong. It rode up my ass, but I was starting to get used to it.

"There she is," Sebastian said. He didn't seem surprised to see me. At least this time Kiki wasn't here with him already.

"I really hate you," I said as I plopped down in a chair across from him. He sat behind his desk, doing who knew what. I slouched down low, not exactly feeling my best. My recent time as Mandi had me feeling particularly low. She was my complete opposite, it seemed. Not to mention the fact she wasn't gay like me. The image of her bouncing on that man's cock where anyone could see her, where anyone could record video of her, still had me reeling.

Sebastian gave me a cock smirk, the kind that only made me more furious. Except, it was now clear to me that there was nothing I could do to him. He probably had it arranged so that all he had to do was push a button and I would transform into Mandi again. He either saw me approach on the security cameras or the bouncer at the front door radioed him.

"Hate me all you want, but you have to admit, I own you now," Sebastian finally said. The worst part was I knew it was true.

"Kiki told me you wanted to see me," I said, hating myself almost as much as I hated him. I had never felt so low. I understood and lived with the hierarchy that existed within the police force. But I didn't like taking orders from others. Only my bosses could order me around. Sebastian was not my boss. He was a leader of a gang. That was all he was. That was all he would ever be.

"She might be dumb, but she's hot and she follows directions," Sebastian commented. "Yes, I wanted to make my offer from earlier more clear."

"Work for you or you keep being a liability to the police I really work for?" I said. "That doesn't seem like a good offer to me. It sounds like crap. You may think you're tempting me or even blackmailing me, but you're really not. I'm just as inclined to tell you to fuck off now as I was this morning."

"Fair enough," Sebastian said. "However, I have decided to revise my earlier offer. I understand the position I have put you in. The truth is, I hadn't intended for you to get in trouble with your bosses like you did. Therefore, I'm going to offer you a deal. There's no reversing what has already been done to you. The closest thing to a cure is a potion I have that regulates the shifting. If you take it, it means you will shift for two days, once per month. It's a bit like the national guard, except you turn into a bimbo instead of a soldier."

"You're lying," I said, not believing a word of what he said. I couldn't trust this man.

"That's a distinct possibility in my line of work," he said, shrugging his shoulders. "It comes with the territory, I suppose. But I can promise you, that if you take the potion, you'll be free of me. And I'll do what I can to take the heat off you with your bosses. You might need to move for a new job, but your trouble here won't hurt your future prospects."

Sebastian knew just where to hit me. He wasn't threatening me, he was offering me a lifeline. And it was one I felt compelled to take. Yes, he might be lying to me, but I was desperate. There was no way I could go back to my old life. My job with the police department was toast. But I wasn't done being a cop yet. I wasn't done being a detective. All I had to do was find a department that would hire me and ignore my past. And if Sebastian could somehow help with that, I'd be set.

"All right," I announced, sitting up and leaning forward, my hand outstretched. "You've got a deal."

After shaking my hand, Sebastian reached into a drawer in his desk and pulled out a bottle filled with a golden liquid. It looked like champagne, but it was something different. I couldn't describe it exactly, but it definitely looked like over-fizzed champagne. He even brought out a champagne flute for me to use to drink it.

"This will take care of you," Sebastian said as he held out the champagne flute. I took it and placed it under my nose, breathing in its vapors. Definitely not champagne.

"Bottoms up," I said as I brought the glass to my lips. Then I started drinking, letting it quickly flow past through my mouth and then down my throat.

As soon as the golden liquid reached my stomach, I started to feel a heat building up inside of me. It felt good. It felt really good.

I was about to ask how long it took to take effect when I looked down and noticed that my top was stretched tighter across my chest than I remembered it before. And then as I watched, right there before my eyes, my breasts expanded, growing bigger and bigger.

"My boobies," I exclaimed, shocked by the sudden growth.

Sebastian laughed. "I told you I wasn't trustworthy. You're going to be my little bimbo fuckdoll from here on out."

"But..." I said, but I couldn't seem to finish my sentence, let alone my thought.

It felt as if all the bubbles in the potion were flowing up into my brain and popping all at once, pushing all those hard thoughts and scary worries out of my head. Those bubbles released pure joy and happiness. My lips turned up into a smile. I couldn't help it. I just felt that good. And I couldn't complain as I continued to watch my boobies grow into a proper pair of titties. They were so big and round.

But it wasn't just my titties that had grown. I could see my lips pushing away from my face, ever so slightly entering my line of sight when I looked down, which I did to watch my titties keep getting bigger. I could feel my ass getting bigger too. My pants had started to feel really tight.

I giggled, wondering why I was wearing such boring clothes. My red sweater looked boring and what kind of bimbo was I to be wearing pants. I wanted people to see my legs and know they could fuck me without a second thought. I didn't even have a first thought to get in the way.

"There she is," Sebastian said. "How's it feel to be a bimbo full time now, Mandi?"

I practically purred before I answered, "I love it." I hugged my body, loving how my big titties felt in my arms. They were so sensitive and they made me horny. Actually, everything made me horny. I was kind of a sex addict now I supposed. But as a bimbo, no one expected anything else from me. And seeing Sebastian smile at my sexy body, I knew everything was going to be perfect from now on. "And I'd love to give you a blowjob."

14

"Yummy," I said as I briefly came up for air. After letting me suck his cock as a way to say thank you for turning me into a bimbo, Sebastian helped me out of my clothes and led me next door to the card room. There wasn't a game going on, but Kiki was sitting there waiting for us.

It took little convincing by Sebastian to get Kiki out of her clothes too. All he had to do was tell her to strip and she started doing it automatically. She didn't even think about it. Ugh, that was hot.

Sebastian had Kiki sit back on the couch on one end. She spread her legs, exposing her bare pussy to me. I couldn't help but lick my lips. I dove in without a second's thought, licking her with all of my worth. Before I knew it, Kiki was running her hands through my long hair, encouraging me as I ate her pretty pink pussy.

But the real fun came when Sebastian got in on the action. I barely heard the sounds of his belt coming loose and then his pants hitting the ground. I definitely felt his fit body climb onto the couch behind me. I understood what he had planned for us.

It was really simple. He was going to fuck me while I ate Kiki's pussy.

And that was exactly what he did. He pushed his big hard cock into my pussy, filling me all the way up on his first thrust. I was wet and ready for him. I was always ready for cock. Deep down, I knew that wasn't always true, but I couldn't help myself now. I loved cock. I lived for cock.

"That's a good bimbo, Mandi," Sebastian said before he slapped my ass.

I jumped up for a moment, but used the opportunity without Kiki's pussy in my face to take a deep breath. But Kiki wasn't to be denied. Her hands forced my head back down and I continued my happy ministrations, licking her pussy and clit, enjoying the taste of her juices as they entered my mouth and dripped down my chin.

I didn't know how it happened, but when Sebastian blasted his second load of cum into me, the first happening back in his office when I sucked his cock, I came too. But even better, Kiki came too. Her thighs clenched around my face as she squirted her juices into my mouth and across my face.

But it was the orgasm that left a permanent mark on me. My whole body convulsed as Sebastian held my hips in his strong hands. Pleasure flowed through me like a giant ocean wave, knowing me back and leaving me dumbfounded. But it felt better than anything ever had before. This was what I was made for. This was my purpose. I was supposed to be sexy and pleasing. And in return I got to cum like a freight train every single time.

I didn't know exactly what Sebastian had planned for Kiki and me. I figured it would be more of the same. I would strip sometimes, which I loved, because it got all those guys to watch my sexy body and throw money at me. And I could always make visits out on the floor or take men who wanted to pay extra back to the VIP rooms for a special show. But sometimes Sebastian would probably want me to entertain at his card games, or be the reward for a job well done by one of his captains. It all sounded so much fun.

But more than anything, I wanted Sebastian to set me up with a woman like I used to be. I wanted to turn her. I wanted to give her the gift that Kiki had given to me. I didn't understand it then, but now I knew the truth. Being a werebimbo is the best. And now that Kiki and I get to live together and serve the sexiest man we know in Sebastian Lambert, life is perfect. He keeps us taken care of, making sure we have lots of sexy clothes to wear to highlight our big tits and bubble butts and he keeps us nice and fucked. Nothing is better.

Someday my old life might catch up to me. People might come looking for Detective Lydia Frost, but even though we share fingerprints, there's nothing else that's left of her. I'm Mandi now and I'm loving the bimbo life.

ABOUT THE AUTHOR

Sadie Thatcher is a longtime author of erotic fiction, especially related to transformations and bimbofication. She likes to say "I have thrown off the shackles of my conservative upbringing and now write erotic stories."

She maintains several blogs devoted to her writings, including a behind the scenes look at her writing process, and bimbos in general, as well as highlights works by other authors. They can be found at:

https://authorsadiethatcher.tumblr.com
https://buildingbettergiggles.tumblr.com

twitter.com/Sadie_Thatcher

ALSO BY SADIE THATCHER

Tales from the Bimbo Ward: Tegan
Tales from the Bimbo Ward: Susan
Tales from the Bimbo Ward: Joy
Tales from the Bimbo Ward: Katherine
Tales from the Bimbo Ward: Sarah
Tales from the Bimbo Ward: Salt and Pepper
Tales from the Bimbo Ward: Amanda
Tales from the Bimbo Ward: The Staff
Mistaken Identity
My New Bimbo Life
Keep Calm and Be a Good Bimbo
(Virtual) Reality
Side Effects
Plaything of Olympus
Experiment in Submission
Bimbo Bet
Snow White and the Evil Witch
Twelve Days of Bimbo
Chosen
The Faerie's Gift
The Bimbo in Yellow
Bad Role Model
Truth or Bimbo
Truth or Bimbo College Edition

Bimbo Dome

Acting the Part

Subliminal Society

Inheritance

Company Morale

His Bimbo Girlfriend

The Bimbo Room

The Bimbos of Blossom

Dr. Jekyll and Missy Hyde

Second Chance

From M&As To T&A

Trading Places

The Bimbo Nutcracker Suite

Milked and Herded

Fitting In

Clowning Around

Transformative Ink

Choices

Rival Competition

Alien Womanhood

Invasion

The Princess and the Bimbo

Bimbo Labyrinth

The Curse of Playing Bimbo Tag

The Curse of Playing Bimbo Tag: Jenna or Jenni

The Bimbo Professor: The Curse of Playing Bimbo Tag Book 3

Anything for the Job

Anything for the Job 2

Anything for His Job

The Bimbo in the Mirror

The Bimbo in the Mirror 2

Astrid and the Bimbo Bee

Bella and the Bimbo Bee

Cali and the Bimbo Bee

Desiree and the Bimbo Bee

Ember and the Bimbo Bee

Fiona and the Bimbo Bee

The Intern

The Lawyer

The Hacker

Cause & Effect

Witless Protection

Stealing Sally

Trial and Error

Beta Testing

Exposed

Simple and Fun Volume 1

Simple and Fun Volume 2

Simple and Fun Volume 3

Simple and Fun Volume 4

Simple and Fun Volume 5

Simple and Fun Volume 6

Bimbo Halloween

Bimbo Christmas

Bimbo Technology

Dorm Room Bimbo

Carissa's Magic Pen

Spirit Walk

Muscle Memory

The Case of the Bimbo Wife

Changes

Changes 2

New Year New You

The Bimbo Dream

The Wedding Gift

The Cure

Backfire

Bim & Bo Yoga

Wishing for Each Other

Bimbo Roots

A Bimbo at Oktoberfest

The Lost Bet

The Fountain

Bimbo Ghost

Sugar and Spice and Everything Nice

Basic Bimbo

A Helping Hand

Bimbos in Space

Christmas Train to Bimboton

Letters to Bimbo Claus

Gone Fishing

The Bimbo Behind the Mask

Rival Wishes

What's in a Name?

Playing the Game

Friendly Wishes

My Chemical Bimbo

To Be Young Again

Something Bimbo Calls Him Home

Wishing for Him

The Author Gets Bimbofied

Body Swap Rings: Happy Anniversary

Body Swap Rings 2: Wedding Night

The Bimbo Experience

The Bimbo Experience 2

The Bimbo Experience 3some

The 4th Bimbo Experience

Bimbo Genes

Bimbo Genes II: The Virus

The Bimbo Genes III: The Epidemic

Bimbo Juice: Blue Raspberry

Bimbo Juice: Grape

Bimbo Juice: Mango

Bimbo Juice: Pineapple

Bimbo Juice: Red Apple

Bimbo Juice: Veggie

Bimbo Juice Gone Wild: The Muse

Bimbo Juice Gone Wild: Street Racer

Bimbo Juice Gone Wild: Score

Bimbos of the Traveling Earrings: Book 1

Bimbos of the Traveling Earrings: Book 2

Bimbos of the Traveling Earrings: Book 3

Bimbos of the Traveling Earrings: Book 4

Bimbo Party: Kennedy

Bimbo Party: Esme

Bimbo Party: Ariana

Bimbo Party: Tara

Workout Buddies

Wishful Thinking

Wanting More

Bimbo Harem: Annabelle

Bimbo Harem: Josie

Bimbo Harem: Nikki

Bimbo Harem: Tiana

Giggle Dust

Giggle Dust 2.0

Giggle Dust 3.0

Giggle Dust 4.0

Bimbo Takeover: The First Step

Bimbo Takeover: Teammates

Bimbo Takeover: Going to the Top

Bimbo Takeover: Revenge of the Bimbos

Thanks for the Mammaries

A New Beginning

Copying Kat

Spreading the Love

Discovering Eden

Building Eden

Spring In Eden

Saving Eden

The Perfect Girlfriend

The Perfect Engagement

The Perfect Wife

The Perfect Woman

Be Hot, Not Smart

No Thoughts for Thots

Be Art, Not Smart

The Cream of the Crop

A New Kind of Passion

Getting the Sugar

A Second Lease on Life

Summer

Autumn

Winter

Spring

Edge for Me

Edge Together

Edge and Deny

The Boutique

Printed in Great Britain
by Amazon